I Won't Cry If Tomorrow Comes

Calvin Markray

I Won't Cry If Tomorrow Comes

Calvin Markray

MILLIGAN BOOKS, INC.

CALIFORNIA

Printed and Bound in the United States of America
Published and Distributed by: Milligan Books

Cover Design: Kevin Allen
Formatting: Milligan Books

First Printing, October 2007
10 9 8 7 6 5 4 3 2 1

ISBN# 978-0-9799308-7-4

Library of Congress Cataloging-in-Publication Data
Markray, Calvin
I Won't Cry If Tomorrow Comes, Calvin Markray

1. Fiction

Milligan Books, Inc.
1425 W. Manchester Ave., Suite C
Los Angeles, California 90047
www.milliganbooks.com
drrosie@aol.com
(323) 750-3592

In Memoriam

For My Mother, Franzella Markray
(1919–1999)

For My Father, Willie D. Markray
(1914-2006)

I WON'T CRY
IF TOMORROW COMES

THE SECRETS WE HOLD
MUST BE REVEALED

IF LIFE IS TO BE SUSTAINED

about the author

CALVIN E. MARKRAY IS A Southern California native who developed an interest in writing dating back to his high school years. In a writing assignment, he was chosen among a host of students to provide a short narrative about life as a high school senior. His work was selected and put in the senior book of essays. Calvin also displayed his craft for acting on stage and being selected to play the lead role *Purlie*, in the stage musical adaption of *Purlie Victorious*. Calvin wrote a three-act play entitled *No More Tears for Mama* that successfully spread to community colleges throughout the greater Los Angeles county area. His first completed and unpublished manuscript, *Dreams Are Only for Heroes*, is yet to come. He has prized himself on selecting *I Won't Cry if Tomorrow Comes* as the groundbreaker for entering the literary world.

dedication

To the most wonderful and inspiring individual that is an important part of my life. Not only did you prevail through the nine long months and pain of ensuring my arrival, you gave me my spiritual connection of knowing it was the inspired anointing of a Higher Source. Thanks, Mom.

And from one rib, they were joined and became one. To the woman who has brought meaning and purpose to my life. Thank you for engaging and indulging yourself in too often an awkward climate of uncertainty. Thank you, my wife, Peg.

acknowledgments

ALL PRAISE AND HONOR TO Him who laid the foundation of the earth in the beginning. Who is man to be counted among the glorious work of Him who created the heavens and the earth? Who spoke and it became? His return is imminent.

To the brother and sisters who shared this dream and journey and inspiration toward the completion of this work (Alvin, Denise, Charlene, Laverne, Willa, Rosie, and Betty).

And they became fruitful and multiplied, bringing forth sons and daughters (Rhonda, Adrian, Carl, Malcom, Kevin, and Calisha).

To my friends—too numerous to name, but not forgotten. You are special people who play a key role in my day-to-day experiences in life. I admire you and appreciate your help in making this journey a rewarding and successful adventure. I consider you as my extended family:

Maria Esquivel, Linda Lopez, Vance Reitz, Alex Gurerro, Anthony Washington, William Simmons, Stephen Nnatchtam, Madeline Bagby, Daryl Thomas, James Martin, Zelma Hatter, Bobby Ramos, Lupo Albano, Rommel Noche, Eduardo Rodriguez, Cipriano Soto, Ronald Kinzanza, Daniel Ibale,

Fernando Valdivia, Sheena Mahmoud, Ernest Clare, Larry Lindberg, Carlos Rosas, Coby Weaver, Darin Reese, Danita Howard, John Johnson and the many others whose names have not been mentioned. THANK YOU!

And special acknowledgements to Dr. Rosie Milligan, Mildred Murphy and Mauderee Gipson.

contents

chapter one

Glitz & Glamour

As the 747 jetliner descended toward Los Angeles International Airport, Toni tilted her head back on her· seat and thought momentarily how it all began. It seemed so long ago—the jubilation and success of a rewarding modeling career. She smiled as she remembered all the different pageants—the other girls. The crowning, the cheers, the flowers, the forever-flashing of camera lights, the thunderous applauses. She remembered the tears flowing down her cheeks—yes, tears of joy and happiness. As she looked out into the sea of jubilant faces, she saw her parents standing and clapping feverishly. Her father blew her a kiss and winked at her while giving her a thumbs-up. Her mother was crying and mouthed, "I love you, baby." Yes, it was a magical night.

Often over time, she recalled someone saying it was like a "Cinderella Story." Toni smiled as she thought, *I never lost a slipper, nor did a young prince come in search of me for a fitting.* Yes, her dream had come true. Her time had finally arrived—all the competitions, the pageants, the modeling interviews, photo-ops. She was acclaimed as "Miss Universe"—the eighth wonder of the world—at least that's what her father would say to her out of love for his daughter. Then, of course, the modeling career began.

The screeching of the plane tires hitting the pavement abruptly brought Toni back to her current state of awareness. She peered out the window, watching the ground crew directing the plane in. She sighed as she heard the voice over the intercom, "Ladies and gentlemen, welcome to Los Angeles. We would like to thank you for flying American. For passengers who are continuing on to San Francisco, there will be a one-hour layover. Once again, thank you for flying American."

Once the plane came to a full stop, passengers immediately jumped out of their seats, retrieving baggage from overhead compartments. Toni sat looking out the window, thinking there was no need to hurry. Passengers struggled with baggage down the aisleway toward the exit of the plane.

"Excuse me, Miss Morrison."

Toni turned to see a smiling female flight atten-dant near her seat.

"Do you need help with your baggage?"

Toni looked at her sheepishly. "You know who I am?"

"Of course, your face is the most recognizable one in the fashion world. I don't think there's a magazine that doesn't have a photo of you on the cover or in it."

Toni smiled, "Thank you, I believe I can man-age."

The attendant moved on down the aisle of the plane as Toni slid out of her seat and reached over-head to retrieve a bag. Suddenly she felt faint. She grabbed the seat to steady herself. Her breath was short, her eyes unfocused. Her head was swirling, going around and around—at least that's what she thought was happening.

Suddenly she felt hands holding her, strong hands, then a voice asking, "Are you alright?"

Toni blinked her eyes to see the face that was before her. "I'm fine, just a little exhausted and jet-lagged."

"You're sure you're okay?" the co-pilot asked.

Toni smiled and nodded, "I'll be fine, thank you."

The young co-pilot looked at her curiously. "Your face looks familiar. I've seen you somewhere before."

The female flight attendant who was standing by quipped, "Only on *every* fashion magazine in the world."

The co-pilot smiled. "Yeah! That's it. You're Toni Morrison, the fashion model. Wow! My pleasure, Miss Morrison." He reached for her baggage. "Let me do the honors."

Toni looking somewhat surprised, she glanced at the female flight attendant. "Charming," she whispered.

The attendant winked, "For the most beautiful woman he's ever seen, he'll probably do somersaults on top·of the plane while flying at thirty-five thousand feet." They both smiled as Toni was escorted from the plane.

Hello Los Angeles

It seemed strange being back in Los Angeles. Everything seemed quite different. Of course, it had been several years since she had last seen her childhood friend, Norma. Toni always thought of her as a sister, a baby sister, in fact. Toni rested in the taxi backseat, taking in the sights as the cab maneuvered its way down Century Boulevard. She noticed the driver looking at her through his rearview mirror.

"Ma'am, are you sure this is the correct address you gave me?"

Toni assumed that he was not originally from this country because he spoke with a heavy accent which she believed was Nigerian. "Unless I tell you otherwise, please go to the address that I've instructed you to, thank you."

The driver made a cautious sigh. "A lady as beautiful as you are, you may want to be very careful. Believe me, Los Angeles may be Disneyland and Hollywood, but it's more Hollyweird and *Dizzy* people."

Toni smiled as she thought for a quick moment, *Could you be a part of it?* Then she felt ashamed for even thinking something like that. After all, he's just trying to make a living. "I'll be just fine, but thank you for your concern."

The cabbie continued looking at her. "Do you play in the movies or something?"

Toni shook her head, "No, I don't play in movies." She gazed out the window observing the people on the streets moving about, going in different directions. Some were rushing and others appeared to be going nowhere, while still others had nowhere to go and seemed resolved with where they were at. She noticed women walking with a swagger up and down the street with weaved hair, knitted stockings, short skirts, revealed breasts, thick mascara, brazen red lipstick, winking coyly at men as they drove by. Several yelled, "Hey, baby, Mama loves you."

A guy yelled back, "Got milk?"

Young Hispanic men stood at corners, holding up bags of oranges. Several Hispanic girls with wide grins offered flowers to motorists. Toni remembered Norma telling her that the Los Angeles vicinity had become heavily Hispanic-populated. As her gaze swept one side of the street to the other, she observed numerous Mexican fast-food outlets. The cab continued to ease down Century, coming to a full stop at Prairie Avenue.

Toni whispered to herself, "Hollywood Park's still standing."

The cabbie, who had a sharp ear and could hear almost anything that seeped out of one's mouth, said, "Yeah, still got some good races every now and then. The Forum is now a church, believe it or not. I remember back in the day that was home to Magic, Karren, Worthy, and the other Lakers. Now we got the Staple Center. To me, it just ain't the same."

Toni thought for a moment about her father, Lester Morrison—the avid, forever-loving Laker's fan. He passed away about five years ago, after losing his beloved wife, Gina Morrison, to breast cancer. Lester was never the same after that—only a shell of himself. Oh, how he loved those Lakers!

Toni hadn't noticed that the cabbie had pulled up in front of a house and stopped. She whispered to herself, "I'm finally here. It's almost unbelievable." It was an attractive, stucco-styled house with a well manicured lawn. The wide living-room window with its drapes drawn back appeared warm and inviting. Toni looked from one side of the street to the other, observing the tall palm trees that lined themselves neatly. She noticed several Mercedes and BMWs in courted driveways. Everything seemed so serene as she recalled Norma telling her how bad the gang problem had become in Los Angeles.

chapter two

Welcome Stranger

T HE CABBIE STOOD BY AS Toni walked to the door and knocked. After a brief moment, the door opened slowly. A little boy who appeared to be about six years of age looked up at her and said, "Hi, my mommy is in the kitchen."

Toni smiled, "Can you tell her that someone is here to see her?"

The little boy scurried off yelling, "Mommy, that lady that played in the *Terminator* is here."

Toni smiled as she thought, *Here we go with the Vanessa Williams thing again.* She recalled on various occasions that she had been told that she resembled Vanessa Williams a lot. She had also been told that she and Halle Berry·could have been linked as kin. Toni heard something break, possibly a dish of some kind. Suddenly, standing before her was Norma, giggling and tearful at the same time. Their eyes met and in a moment she was taken back to a time that would never be forgotten. Toni's eyes·watered as they both embraced each other. Norma squeezed her hard, and Toni gasped for air.

"Look at you," Norma said, stepping back to admire Toni.

"Oh my God, it's really you."

At that moment, the cabbie blew his horn. They both turned toward the street to hear him say, "I got a living to make. I can't stand here all day."

Norma frowned, "Just hold your horses, buddy."

The cabbie let out a loud sigh. Norma took Toni's hands and squeezed them. "I can't believe it's really you. Pinch me or something."

Toni kissed her on the cheek. "It's really me, after all this time."

Again the cabbie blew his horn. "Sorry, but I got to go."

Toni stepped away from Norma, "Girlfriend, let me pay this man before he drives off with my luggage." Toni paid the cabbie and thanked him. He nodded appreciatively when she tipped him a twenty-dollar bill. Happily, he blew his horn and drove away.

For several more moments they just stood there acknowledging each other. Then Norma wrapped her arm in Toni's arm and both proceeded into the house. "Girl, you're still just as beautiful as ever.

I always said that when the good Lord gave out beauty, you must have been the first one in line." They both giggled.

Toni took Norma's hands and stepped back. "Girl, looks as if you might have put on a pound or two."

Norma battered her eyes. "What can I say? Marriage is good." She ushered Toni toward the sofa. "Let me have your coat; take off your shoes, girl. You home now."

Toni stood for a moment admiring Norma's home. "Girl, this is really a beautiful home. You've got it so nicely decorated."

Norma chuckled, "With those three little monsters I got, believe me, I stay on the go. Girl, we got so much catching up to do. You want some tea or coffee? Have you eaten anything? I mean, real food, not that stuff they give you on the plane."

Toni rubbed her hands together, "I'm fine, just a little jet-lagged. Where are the boys and James?"

Norma nodded in the direction of the entertainment room, "Playing videos or something. James will be getting off work shortly."

Toni looked at the mantel that had a picture of her and Norma when they were in high school. She walked over and picked up the picture as she smiled and shook her head. "It's almost hard to believe that the years have gone by. We were so young, so innocent, and somewhat foolish too, I guess."

Norma nodded in agreement. "Yep, but we had some great times. If I could, I wouldn't change any of it for the world." That said, they both sat on the sofa, smiling at each other.

"Girlfriend, tell me about all your accolades. I know you've traveled all over the world, gone to exotic places, met beautiful people. I just want to know what it's like to be famous with all the trimmings. I got magazines all over my bedroom with you in them. James teases me all the time saying he married the wrong girl. He just doesn't know how lucky he is to have me." They both laughed. "So come on, Toni, tell me about everything. Start with the real juicy stuff first—like have you met Mr. Right?"

Toni shook her head. "Norma, believe me, it's not quite what it may appear to be. I must say in many ways I've been truly blessed, sometimes far more than I ever expected. But having the things of the world doesn't fill the void, the emptiness that one endures. Even as a kid I always wanted to know what a glamorous life-style would be like. Of course, I worked hard to get where I ultimately got to, but it's not the same. Sometimes I'm happy, other times I'm not sure about anything. I know that I've missed you and wanted you to share in my success. However, I realize that you need your space to do whatever it is that brings you happiness. And by your looks, you've done it well."

Norma looked at Toni somewhat puzzled. "Girlfriend, the whole world is yours. Every time you step out on a stage, the world stops. You're Toni Morrison, Miss Excitement."

Toni dropped her head into the palms of her hands. Quickly, Norma moved over to her and put her arm around her. "What is it, girlfriend? I'm here. You can talk to me."

Toni lifted her head as tears rolled down her cheeks. "I'm so tired, Norma."

Norma believing that Toni was speaking about the air flight, attempted to console her by letting her know that her room was ready. "Toni, I know it's been hard and difficult for you since you lost your mom and dad, but, girlfriend, you still got family. I'll always be here for you, no matter what. Remember, I'm your sister and that's for life."

Norma stood up, "Look, you've had a long flight and you're tired. Go rest for a while and when you feel better, you might want to take a hot bath, relax those muscles, get the tension off of you."

Toni arose to her feet somewhat wobbly and reached for Norma for balance. Norma put her arm around her waist to steady her. "Toni, are you sure you're alright?"

Toni managed a slight smile. "Jet-lag I suppose." She took a shower, then lay down on the inviting bed as Norma went to make a cup of hot tea for her. In a moment, Toni found herself in a fog of heavy slumber. Norma came to the room to see her best friend engulfed in deep sleep. She smiled as she sipped the tea she had made for Toni and thought, *Poor baby.*

Toni struggled in her sleep, but the dreams kept reappearing. The faces—that awful place. Then *him*—a face she did not want to recognize any more. But there was another face, too, a beautiful, small, round face with twinkling eyes. Her mother's face appeared, softly telling her to do the right thing. Her father's face appeared, asking, "Where is the child?" Her lover's face cried out, "How could you?" She turned and rolled frantically. She heard herself begging, pleading, "Please stop!"

The next moment she was in Paris, then Rome, then Spain, Hawaii, New York, leaving the Trump Towers and entering a waiting limo. Driven to photo shoots, preparing to appear on late-night talk shows. Entering hotels through guarded entrances, away from the cameras and onlookers. Head swirling, tense, agitated, wanting—needing—that moment alone. All she wanted was a moment of peace, a little quiet, some solitude.

The weight gain, moody, morning sickness, strange appetite, swollen feet—"My career, my career," she moaned. "My career will be over." The hideaway, her secret place—at least until the pregnancy was over. The baby. Can't have the baby. Save the baby.

chapter three

Good Morning All

Toni lay in bed, listening to the chirping of the birds outside the bedroom window. In an afterthought, it appeared as if they were trying to tell her something. There was a ray of sunlight, yet the sky appeared cloudy with the threat of rain. She closed her eyes for a brief moment and saw herself back in New York, at the Waldorf Hotel. She immediately opened her eyes when she heard a voice say, "My mommy cooking breakfast." She turned to see little Eric standing in the doorway.

"Well, good morning to you, sir. You're up bright and early," Toni smiled. Suddenly, Norma appeared in the doorway behind little Eric. "Boy! Go wake up your father and your brothers. Toni's trying to rest."

Toni smiled somewhat appreciatively. "It's okay, girlfriend. I was preparing to get up anyway. Smells awfully good. Somebody has been busy this morning in the kitchen, I see."

Norma nodded toward the kitchen. "Whenever you're ready, come on in there and let me fix you a nice breakfast. Now I need to go and check on the other two little terrors. Got to get them washed up and fed and ready for church."

Toni pointed her finger at Norma. "You go, Supermom."

After Norma left, she sat on the edge of the bed, observing the bedroom. It was so neatly arranged. It really made her feel so welcomed. Toni stood and looked at herself in the full-length door mirror. She still had that girlish figure. Not quite the figure she had when she was modeling, but good enough to tease any crowd of onlookers who would welcome her to stroll down any aisleway. Her face was as beautiful and elegant as ever. Even the sadness that lay hidden behind those piercing eyes did not extract an ounce of glamour from her face.

Tears began to slowly trickle down her cheeks. She asked herself, "Why? Oh, God, why?" Slowly walking into the bedroom bath, Toni took her toothbrush, put paste on it, and started brushing vigorously. She looked in the mirror at her long, richly flowing hair that fell well beneath her shoulders. Somewhat refreshed, she wrapped her robe around her sleek body and started toward the kitchen, where she saw Norma busily preparing plates with scrambled eggs, sausages, toast, and fried slices of tomatoes. The aroma from the coffee instantly made one take a deep breath. Chilled glasses of orange juice looked inviting, sitting on the table.

"Wow! This looks scrumptious," Toni exclaimed, standing with her arms folded while looking at Norma.

Norma turned to Toni, "Girlfriend, go have a seat at the dining table and I will be serving your highness in a minute."

Toni shook her head, "You know, Norma, I've missed you so much and feel so guilty about not coming to see you or write as often as I should. But my world has been a turmoil of sorts. Right after 9/11, things seemed to have changed. It was as if I were losing control of my life."

"Oh, nonsense," Norma replied while setting a plate before Toni. "Girl, you had a career that kept you running and hopping out of airplane seats that spanned across the world. All those pageants, modeling assignments, photo shoots, presentations, being a spokesperson for different magazines. You worked hard to achieve success, and you're entitled to everything you got."

Toni felt a cold chill go down her spine as she thought, *Everything I got—but what do I really have?*

At that moment, James and the boys arrived at the dining room table. James smiled cordially, "Good morning, Toni! Did you sleep well last night?"

Toni smiled, "Good morning, James! I was very comfortable, thank you."

James looked at his sons. "Fellows, say good morning to Ms. Morrison."

In unison, the children said good morning while attempting to seat themselves comfortably.

Toni smiled. "They are so precious. How old are you, Eric?"

He ignored her for a moment, looking at the contents of what lay before him on his plate. James tapped the table lightly, "Eric, Ms. Morrison is speaking to you, son."

Eric didn't look up. Still eyeing what was on his plate, he said, "I'm seven, Corey is five, and him," pointing at Lil' Jay, "him is three."

Toni looked from one to the others, "You're all handsome young men."

Corey looked at his dad. "I'm a little boy, my dad's a man." James shook his head and smiled.

Norma placed a plate of pancakes, toast, sausage, and a pitcher of orange juice on the table.

Eric looked at her, "Mom, I don't want scramble eggs. Can I have Froot Loops?"

Corey and Lil' Jay yelled in unison, "We want Froot Loops too."

Toni put her hand to her mouth, not wanting to show the grin that was spreading across her face. James looked at the boys somewhat sternly. "Eat what your mother put on your plate or no ice cream after church." The three boys looked at each other and sighed in surrender. Norma set a hot cup of tea before Toni.

"Girlfriend, you better eat something."

Toni took the cup of tea to her mouth and blew into it. "So what's on the agenda for today?" she said, looking at Norma.

Norma shrugged. "Church, then dinner, I guess. We all could go for a ride somewhere after dinner; then again, these boys will be so out of it by then that it'll be their bedtime. I know you must still be exhausted, but you're more than welcome to come with us. A little spiritual enlightenment might do you some good. The service is really invigorating."

Toni noticed that everyone at the table was looking at her. She puckered her lips. "I know I should really, but on the other hand, I think I'll pass." Norma and James looked at each other, somewhat surprised.

Toni rose from the table, "I think I'll take a hot shower to relieve some of the tension." She exited from the dining area to her room.

James sipped his coffee. "She seems a little out of it, like something is wrong or missing."

Norma casually chewed a piece of toast. "She's just tired and probably needs some time alone."

James sighed. He finished his coffee. "I'm gonna shower. You might want to get a jump-start with the boys. You know it almost takes a month of Sundays to get them dressed. He kissed Norma on the forehead and walked to their bedroom. Just at that moment, Corey threw some eggs at Eric and giggled. "I got you! I got you!"

Norma looked at them both and said, "Behave, both of you." She looked towards Toni's bedroom and thought, *Something's not right.* After an hour or so, Norma peered into Toni's bedroom to find her asleep. Norma smiled as she thought, *Girlfriend is really tired.* Then they left for church.

chapter four ■■■■■■■■■■

Dreams

TONI AWOKE VISIBLY SHAKING, PERSPIRATION rolling down from her forehead. Tears clouded her eyes. She folded her arms and rocked back and forth, whispering as if speaking to someone who might have been relatively close by—yet not near enough to reach out and touch. "Mom, Dad, I need you. Please help me." She lay back and curled her knees to her chest. The memories of when she was a child and would suck her thumb for relief flooded back to her. She closed her eyes. Immediately she recalled when she fell while skating as a little girl, bruising her knee. Tears flowed down her cocoa-buttered cheeks as she sought her father, who was standing on the porch of their home with outstretched arms, waiting for her.

"Come to daddy, my little angel," she could hear him say. She ran to him, forgetting the pain, and leaped into his arms.

"It hurts, Daddy," she cried, looking into his somber blue eyes, waiting for the right words to come from him, knowing that they would bring comfort. In that moment, she saw her black mother standing behind her father. Her smile genuine, her beauty enhanced by her love for both of them, her white man and her exceptionally beautiful daughter.

Within a moment, her parents' faces faded away, to be replaced by another face—a white face that she tried not to see anymore. A face that did not offer the same warmth and gentleness that was seen and expressed oftentimes in the face of her father. This face brought pain, agony, distress, and fear. This face placed her in an awkward position.

Once again, there were the oohs, the aahs, the smiles, some inviting, others with disdain—particularly among the women.

Now the image was of a sea of lights that came repeatedly from the cameras. She remembered the well-dressed men and women around her. The men examined·her with lustful eyes, savoring the thought of spending one night with her—possibly more nights than one. She walked down the runway gracefully, swaying her hips, her head erect, shoulders squared, and feet gliding along. Stopping, swirling, glancing around, her perfectly white teeth tantalizing others through her sensuous, cherry-rose lips, revealing a smile that could be auctioned for a million dollars. Her hair radiant, gleaming as it sashayed from one shoulder to the other. Her eyes were radiant emerald green speckled with brown. The spaghetti straps of her gown seductively hung from·her shoulders.

She was fascinating—a wondrous sight to behold. As she gracefully moved back toward center stage, she observed a gentleman sitting near the platform with a confident smile on his face. He nodded at her, and she felt butterflies in her stomach. He was a handsome-looking fellow and drew her eyes like a magnet. At center stage, she turned to the audience. Hands on her hips, she looked from left to right, gave a sultry kiss, a wink of the eye. The applause was thunderous, the whistling enthusiastic. Shouts of "Yes! Yes! You're sensational!" echoed as she left the stage, heading to her dressing room. Still she could hear the applause of the people.

❧ ❧ ❧

Fully awake now, Toni focused on her present surroundings. She realized that she was still in bed. She thought to herself, *I have to do this. I must do this now. Too many years have gone by.* With that, she hurriedly pulled her luggage from the closet and started packing.

As more uninvited thoughts roamed through her head, Toni, sobbing, could only utter, "Oh my God! What have I done? I must have been insane."

chapter five ━━━━
The Long Journey

TONI QUICKLY DRESSED, CALLED, AND confirmed that she could get a flight out to Miami in the next several hours. She hated herself for doing what she was doing, knowing it wasn't fair to Norma, yet she knew it had to be done—she was on a path from which she could not deviate. Before calling a cab, she sat at the dining room table with pen and pad. Her eyes began to moisten as she began to write.

"Dear Norma,

I really don't know how to begin this. I guess I can start by saying I'm so sorry if I've inconvenienced you and your family in any way. There was so much I wanted to share with you about my life over the years. There are things that I believe only you would understand. So much has happened. At present, I can only say that I'm on a mission—a mission that I hope to share with you and even the world. I love you and your family very much and hope to be a part of you all when this journey is complete. Give James and the boys my love. Stay strong, stay whole, stay the course. I will write or phone you along the way. Please try and understand. Best wishes.

Love,
Toni

TONI CALLED A cab.

⚛ ⚛ ⚛

THE BOYS GLEEFULLY got out of the car and chased one another in the yard. Norma looked back at them. "Okay, you guys, don't be running near the streets." As she entered the house she looked towards Toni's bedroom. "Hey, girlfriend, you up yet?" Receiving no answer, Norma started towards the bedroom when James called to her, "Honey, I think you better come and read this."

Norma walked over to James, looking at the dismayed expression on his face. In his hand was a piece of paper. He handed it to her and shook his head as he walked into the kitchen. Norma began to read the note. When she was finished, she gasped for air, then sat down dejectedly in the chair at the dining room table. She picked up the note and attempted to read it again, trying to get a clearer understanding exactly what Toni was saying, or trying to say. James stood in the doorway of the kitchen. He looked at his wife and felt a sudden loss for her. Walking over to her, he gently put his arm around her shoulder until she looked up at him, wanting answers, but he had none to give. A tear rolled down her cheek. "I don't understand!" she whispered.

જી જી જી

IT ALL SEEMED so familiar. Here she was once again, airborne. Flying, flying, it seemed like forever, flying all through her career. Flying from one place to another. Toni thought to herself, *No wonder I don't feel normal.* Her career was over, and yet she was still flying. But in her heart, she knew why she was still flying. She was on a mission—one that she hoped would end successfully. She thought momentarily, *Is this an illusion?* then she sighed. All she could think of was *Am I losing my mind?*

Toni stared out the window, taking in the soft, white, puffy clouds as they ever so increasingly seemed to drift by the wing of the plane. A smile came over her face as she imagined seeing two angels with fully extended wings flying near the plane. They had a finger pointed straight ahead, looking at her with no expression at all.

Toni was distracted by, "Are you comfortable, Ma'am? Can I get anything for you?"

She turned to see a smiling female flight attendant. "Oh, thank you. I'm just fine. When will we be arriving in Miami?"

The attendant looked at her watch. "Approximately one hour and fifty-five minutes."

"Thank you," Toni replied as she turned to gaze once again out the window. She strained her eyes. "Where are the angels?" she whispered to herself. The plane bumped, buckled, and shimmied a bit, leaving some passengers with heavy "aahs" and "oohs." Toni looked across the aisle to see a smiling woman who appeared to be in her mid- to late-fifties.

She nodded at Toni, "A little turbulence, I suppose."

Toni smiled reluctantly. "I guess." The woman had a book in her hand. Toni couldn't see the title of the book, so she asked, "What's the name of the book you're reading?"

The woman held the book up for Toni to see. "It's *The Long Journey Home*, by Os Guinness."

Toni nodded. "Pretty good?"

The woman smiled. "It's wonderful. I've read four chapters since our flight. Is the seat next to you taken?"

Toni looked at the empty seat. "The gentleman who was sitting here has been gone for a while."

chapter six

Confronting Self

THE LADY ROSE FROM WHERE she sat and seated herself next to Toni. "If he comes back, I'll just get up and move back to my seat. My, you're such a beautiful girl."

Inwardly, Toni cringed, thinking to herself, *I hope I haven't given her the belief that I'm in dire need for conversation.* Instead, she smiled and said, "Thank you."

Once she positioned herself more comfortably in the seat, the woman extended her hand towards Toni. "My name is Julia Pearsol. Everyone calls me Julie."

Toni took her hand and squeezed it gently. "I'm Toni Morrison."

"Well, Miss Morrison, or is it *Mrs.* Morrison?"

"It's Miss Morrison," Toni replied.

"I can't believe some lucky, handsome fellow hasn't fallen all over himself to get you down that aisle of holy matrimony." She patted Toni on her hand. "Anyway, my dear, I'm going to tell you a little about the novel I'm reading." She leaned towards Toni. "I could swear I've seen your face somewhere before."

Toni shrugged, "Maybe a look-alike?"

The woman cocked her head slightly, "No, dear. God only makes beauty one time like you. Anyway, the book is about a beautiful young girl, much like yourself. She's looking for her parents, who gave her up for adoption. She feels her life is incomplete until she finds them."

She turned to Toni to see tears streaming down her face. "Oh, dear, sweetheart, what's wrong? Are you okay?"

Toni began to sob. "Please, please ..."

The woman became visibly shaken as she looked around for an attendant. A young man walked by and noticed. "Is everything okay here?"

The woman looked at him sternly. "You idiot, can't you see she's upset? Go get an attendant."

The young man quickly left. In a moment, a flight attendant was standing beside them. "Is there a problem?"

The woman looked at the attendant admonishingly. "Can't you see she's upset? Go get some water or something. By the way, bring me a glass of gin, two of those small bottles." The attendant started to move, but the woman pulled at her arm. Looking around, she cautioned, "Dear, no ice in the gin."

The attendant looked startled until the woman said in an authoritative demeanor, "Go!"

In a moment, Toni was sipping water from a bottle and dabbing her eyes. The stranger put an arm around her shoulder. "It's alright, honey, just let it all out. I'm here for you."

Toni looked at the woman with baffled eyes. "You don't even know me. You have no idea what has happened."

The woman squeezed Toni's shoulder. "Whatever it is, I'm here for you—to help you."

Toni looked at her in a startled and grave way. "Who are you? What do you want from me?" The woman shifted in the seat. "I'm going to help you."

Toni looked at her for a long moment. "You can't help me. Nobody can help me."

The woman assured her and said, "Sweetheart, I see your pain. I'm sure it's frustrating. But you *must* continue the journey. The answers will come. You must not give up. Behind every door is a secret. You must find the key to unlock that door to reveal its hidden treasure."

The woman was interrupted with, "Excuse me; I believe this is my seat."

Both Toni and the woman both looked up to see a gentleman standing by. "Oh, I'm sorry," the woman said, rising from the seat. She patted Toni on the shoulder. "You're going to be fine, my dear." With those final words, she crossed the aisle back to her own seat. Toni stared at her, confused.

The gentleman seated himself, buckled in, and exhaled. "What a long flight."

Toni continued to stare at the woman, who smiled and winked her eye at Toni. Toni averted her attention directly ahead, but her heart was pounding rapidly. She took several deep breaths, trying to calm her nerves.

The gentleman turned to her. "After all these years of flying around the world and throughout the nation, my nerves still get rattled when I fly. By the way, I'm Doctor Feldman."

Toni didn't bother to reply as she only heard "I'm Doctor—I'm Doctor—I'm Doctor Richards. You may have six months—six months—six months to live." Toni almost wanted to scream, "Stop it! Stop it, please!"

The doctor was startled by the look on her face. "I'm sorry, I didn't mean anything."

Toni turned to him, "Oh, I'm sorry. I was just thinking. Please forgive me." Although she smiled benignly at her companion, her thoughts raced back to her physician's cutting words when he recently told her about her malignant, genetic blood condition that was life-threatening which had shaken her to her core.

The doctor nodded with approval. "I guess long flights can take a toll," he said softly as he looked at Toni with eyebrows knitted together in surprise.

Toni's mind was in a fog as she vaguely heard a voice say, "Ladies and gentlemen, take your seats, please. Fasten your seat belts. We will be landing shortly."

chapter seven

Arriving in Miami

THE PLANE LANDED WITH A thud. "My goodness," Toni mumbled to herself. Her mind was racing, thinking of all the things she wanted to do—needed to do. For a moment, she felt a tinge of guilt, leaving Los Angeles, leaving Norma behind without taking the time to really talk with her. She felt ashamed, but there was something gnawing inside of her, relentlessly pushing her forward, making her aware of the need to move on.

She spoke to herself as she entered the terminal. "I must keep going—time—so little time—so much ground to cover." She was startled when a voice with a Spanish accent asked, "You need help with your bags, lady?" Toni turned to her right to see a tanned, black, curly-haired youngster smiling, showing a set of uneven teeth.

Toni smiled somewhat nervously. "Thank you, but I'll manage."

The youngster moved towards her. "Well, let me get you a cab." Before Toni could reply, he whistled for a cab, picked up her bags, and waited to place them in it when the cab arrived.

The cabbie got out of the vehicle, opened the trunk, and eagerly reached for her luggage. However, the young man looked at him sternly. "I got it for the lady."

The cabbie looked at Toni with a slight frown. Toni smiled nervously. "It's okay. I'm sure he can place them in the trunk." The cabbie nodded as he scornfully looked at the youngster.

After the bags were safely placed in the trunk, Toni handed the young man a five dollar bill. To her astonishment, he yelled, "You think I'm some poor beggar? You think I need your money?"

With an air of pride, he reached into his pants pocket and pulled out a handful of crumpled bills. "You see this? I have money, pretty lady. But you feel sorry for Ernesto, yes? I don't need your money."

Toni was startled. She didn't know how to respond. She tried to put on a casual smile. "I didn't mean to offend you in any way. I was just showing my appreciation for your help." The youngster smiled, casting his eyes to the ground. "You are a beautiful lady. A princess—a rare jewel. If you wanted me to, I would carry your baggage anywhere."

Toni felt flattered. "That's awfully nice of you. You're a real gentleman."

The youngster looked at Toni. "You like Ernesto?"

Toni looked over at the cabbie, who was shaking his head. "Ernesto, I think you are a nice person; however, I must be going now."

Toni got in the cab and as it pulled from the curb, she looked back at the lonely figure that stood gazing at her. She felt a loss for the youngster, yet she believed that he was a survivor and he would make it.

After arriving at the hotel, Toni felt totally exhausted. She longed for a hot shower, a little slumber. She sat on the edge of the queen-size bed, taking in the contents of the room. Slowly, she got up to get the TV remote and turned on the set to nothing in particular. In complete disinterest of the television's offerings, she walked to the sliding glass door and pulled back the drapes. The view was striking. It drew her out onto the balcony, where she looked down at the traffic and noticed tiny people casually going about their way. From her sixteenth-floor room looking toward the beach, the view was breathtaking. A slight breeze blew, perfuming the air with the tropical scent of lilac.

"A hot shower, a nap, then some dinner," Toni whispered to herself. "Then it's time to set things in motion."

She began to undress while a multitude of things ran through her mind. As she stood naked, looking at herself in the closet mirror, she admired her own body, thinking how she had managed to keep it shapely over the years. Her hand went to her stomach as she thought back, *I carried you for nine months and in just a few moments, I gave you up, gave you away.* Her eyes moistened. "I'll find you. I swear I'll find you. Then I'll tell you why. I'll answer all the questions that I know you will have for me. I'll tell you that I'm sorry—even though I know 'sorry' will not be enough. I'll tell you that I love you, even though you may not believe it."

Toni was startled by a knock at the door. Reaching for her robe, she called out, "Yes?"

A male voice answered, "Room service, Ma'am."

Quickly tying the robe around her, she thought, *I didn't order any room service.*

She wiped her eyes. "Just a moment."

Walking to the door and peering through the peephole, Toni saw a young man dressed in hotel attire, holding a bouquet of flowers. It was evident that he was a hotel employee. She opened the door to see the smiling young man standing tall and erect.

"Ms. Morrison, compliments of the hotel." He extended the flowers towards her along with a bottle of champagne.

Toni smiled, "Why, thank you."

"My pleasure, Ma'am," he said, almost fidgeting.

"Wait. I have something for you," Toni said smiling, thinking that a ten dollar tip would be nice for him.

"No need, Ma'am. As I said, compliments of the hotel." He saluted her and walked away like a well-disciplined soldier. Toni closed the door and walked to the mantel, where she placed the flowers. She looked at the bottle of champagne and marveled, "Nice." Seeing a vase on the dresser, she retrieved it, put the flowers in it, and took a shower.

As the beads of water peppered her body, again her thoughts were of her modeling days. She thought of the other girls who, like herself, competed and yearned for the admiration of others, who basked in the camera lights, whose ears were tickled as they listened to the oohs and aahs of adoring masses, who relished the applause, the jubilation, the possibilities. Once again, in that moment, she felt faint. However, she steadied herself against the shower wall and took several deep breaths. Shaking her head gingerly, she reached for the luxurious bath towel and began to pat herself dry. As she walked to the bed and sat down, reaching for her lotion on the dresser, a voice on the TV stated, "There are so many children in adoption centers that need a home. Could *you* love a child enough to want to give him or her a home?"

chapter eight

Play It Again

TONI KNEW SHE HAD TO play it back again in her mind. She didn't want to, but knew she had to. *Why once again?* she thought, when it's been in her head for years. She had lived with it for so long, yet, it was as haunting as if it happened only yesterday. It's something every woman who has ever experienced such an ordeal would like to forget—*totally* forget. *It's in the past,* she thought. But was it really? The past can produce results that sustain themselves into one's future. For the eleven-hundredth time, she asked herself, "Why me? What did I do to deserve this?" She tried desperately to make logic of things, hoping, like many times before, it was a dream, only a dream. But she knew in her heart it was a nightmare she had to encounter once again. Her second mind told her "put it in a box, tape it, store it away—*far* away." But reality challenged her:

"Truth, fight for the truth, fight to live." Like a movie playing in slow-motion, Toni went back—back to the beginning—that awful night over five years ago.

It was a beautiful spring night. A night of sweet aromas floating on soft breezes. Toni sat in her dressing room admiring the roses and other flowers that were sent by well-wishers and admirers. She was distracted by a knock on the door. "Yes?" she answered.

"Toni, it's me, Liz. May I come in?"

"Certainly," Toni replied.

Liz Bolton opened the door and peered in, smiling, extending her hands toward Toni. "Honey, you were just *fabulous* tonight. You knocked them off their feet. Oh, this New York crowd is tantalizing. The mayor and his wife were invigorated by you, darling. Oh, Toni! Sweetheart, you're just gorgeous. There's an after-party at Trump Plaza, and *everyone* is expecting you. Brad and Angelina are going to be there, and I hear that Denzel may show. There are several up-and-coming young models who would like to meet you, too."

Toni breathed deeply and tried to give a genuine smile. "Liz, any other time I would be more than ready to oblige. But I feel like I need a little time to myself. You understand, don't you?"

Liz, standing with her hands on her hips, looked at Toni with pure admiration. "Of course, I do, sweetheart. I'll just tell everyone you had a terrible headache and needed to rest a bit. Don't worry. I'll take care of everything. By the way, I'll have the driver pull up to the side door. That way you don't have to exit from the front entrance. There're photographers everywhere."

"No, no," Toni almost snapped. "No driver. I'm going to walk. The hotel is just several blocks, and it will do me good."

Liz looked startled as she clasped her hands to her chest. *"Walk?!"* she exclaimed. "Sweetheart, surely you're kidding! Toni, you're a celebrity. You just don't *walk* anywhere. There are people who wait on you hand and foot. I wouldn't dare let you walk anywhere. Oh, my goodness! This is unbelievable. You're kidding, right?"

Toni looked into Liz's surprised and startled eyes. "I'm not kidding, Liz. I just want a few moments alone—to myself. I want to breathe for a moment. I want to feel like a normal person. I'll be fine. What could ever happen to Toni Morrison, world-renowned fashion model?"

Liz's eyes watered as she studied Toni. "I've been with you all these years, watched you grow into the most beautiful person that I've come to know. You're like a daughter to me. When you took me on as a consultant, I never dreamed our lives would entwine as they did when my modeling career ended a while back. As I got older, I felt the world had forgotten all about me. Then there you were—young, vibrant, beautiful, energetic. You reminded me so much of myself." Tears freely flow down Liz's cheeks.

Toni stood and embraced her. "Liz, I love you dearly. You've always been there for me. Without you, I would not be where I am today. Tell me you understand, 'cause deep in your heart, I believe that you do."

Toni finished by looking her straight in the eye and saying, "I *promise* I'll be alright." She smiled broadly, "And I won't talk to strangers along the way."

Liz kissed Toni on the forehead, "You're such an angel. Well, if you insist, I'll have the bodyguard standby. At least he can tag along—out of sight, out of mind. I'll feel better knowing Malcom will be close. I'll let him know. Sweetheart, please don't be out too long. You need to get some rest. It's been one hectic year. At least we can look forward to that two-week vacation in the Bahamas."

Toni nodded in agreement. "Liz, go to the party and enjoy yourself. Everything will be just fine."

Liz walked to the door, then turned towards Toni with arms folded. Quickly, Toni put up a finger to her lips as if indicating to Liz not to speak another word. "Go! I'll be fine." Liz left. Toni sat back in the chair, facing the mirror.

chapter nine

An Unannounced Visitor

TONI WONDERED HOW HER MOM and dad were doing. She hadn't spoken to either of them in almost two weeks. She was concerned about them, although she knew they were just fine. Glancing at the clock on the wall, then the phone, she asked herself, "I wonder if they're asleep, or even home?" Of course, there was a three-hour difference between the East and West Coast.

A sudden knock at the door shook her out of her reverie. Believing it was Liz again, Toni answered, "Liz, I'm fine."

A strong masculine voice responded, "Miss Morrison, it's me, Malcom."

She replied "Come in."

Malcom entered and his presence seemed to have taken up most of the room. He was about six-feet-five and weighed almost two-ninety. His physical attributes—meaning his massive arms, broad shoulders, and barrel chest—made him appear to be *very* intimidating. He had hands that looked to be the size of a professional baseball player's glove. His face, however, showed warmth, accompanied by a sly smile.

"Liz, Ms. Bolton, that is, said that I'm to accompany you on your evening stroll."

Toni nodded, "Yes, that's correct. However, I would appreciate it if you wouldn't make it so obvious. Maybe ... like walking fifty feet behind me."

Malcom's right brow rose a bit in incomprehension. "I don't quite understand."

Toni turned towards the mirror and breathed heavily. "I just need some space. I just want to share me with *me* for a moment."

Malcom looked a little puzzled. "I didn't mean anything other than I want you to understand I'm here to do my job—that's all."

Toni smiled, "I know you take your job very seriously. That's good, Malcom. Look, I'll be dressed momentarily, then you can do your job. Why don't you go to the lounge, have a drink, and by that time, I should be ready."

Malcom nodded as he backed to the door. "Yes, Miss Morrison, that'll be fine." He left.

Toni felt a pounding in her head. *A headache coming on for sure*, she thought. She began to undress when suddenly, there was another knock at the door. She quickly robed and almost screamed, "What is it?"

A voice, calm, steady, reserved, almost a whisper, said, "Miss Morrison, my name is Jean Plushette. May I have a moment with you?"

Toni, being somewhat inquisitive, recognized that the voice had a French accent. "I'm sorry, I don't have the time. I'm preparing to leave."

There was a moment of silence, then the voice spoke again. "Just one moment, Mademoiselle. Please, I beg of you."

Toni quickly looked at herself in the mirror before opening the door. She was about to speak to the intruder, but before her stood the most striking, incredible, handsomest man that she had ever seen. Toni was mesmerized by the sparkle of his eyes. His intriguing smile could only be matched by her very own. He was speaking, yet not a word was coming from his mouth. He gently placed a bouquet of roses to her chest. Without realizing it, Toni protectively folded her arms across the bouquet to ensure they would not fall to the floor. He stepped past her nonchalantly.

Toni, still mesmerized, turned only after she heard him say, "Mademoiselle Morrison, I must say, you were quite royal—beyond description—tonight. In all the splendor of beauty, your elegance surpasses the infinite creation of the world. *Fantastique!*"

Toni's mind was boggled. It cleared just enough to ponder the question, *What was he saying? What IS he saying?* then in that moment, Toni remembered his face. *Yes! He was the intriguing gentleman who sat nearest to the platform. That smile, the confidence he wore.*

Toni ran her fingers through her hair nervously. "I'm glad you enjoyed the performance. Now, if you would excuse me, I have to change."

He walked over to her and gently placed his hand on her shoulder. She felt a tingling sensation move through her body that she identified as an electric current. "You're a very beautiful woman," he said, studying her reflection in the mirror. "I would like to take you to dinner. Something light; after all, I know it's getting late."

Toni removed his hand from her shoulder. "Thank you. That's awfully nice, but I really must change and get going."

He stared at her sensuously. "Perhaps I can have my limo pick you up?"

Toni's lower lip began to quiver, "Really, I do have another engagement."

"Very well," he said as he moved to the door, "perhaps I'll see you another time."

Toni lowered her head and wrestled with the conflicting emotions she was experiencing as he walked out and quietly closed the door.

chapter ten

The Encounter

TONI RUBBED HER HAND ACROSS her forehead. Beads of perspiration bathed her skin. Her head was throbbing. She put the fingers of both hands to her temple and began to massage ever so gently. *I need to get some air.* After dressing, she looked around to find her purse, dimmed the lights, and walked out the door. Near the theatre entrance she heard, "Miss Morrison, are you leaving now?"

Toni turned to see Malcom, her assigned bodyguard, waiting nearby. She stared at him for a moment, awed that he looked so Goliath-like—menacing, yet humble.

"I'm going to walk to the hotel, Malcom. I'll be fine. Why don't you go and enjoy the rest of the evening?"

Malcom looked at her with a raised brow. "But Liz told me to make sure you get to the hotel safely."

Toni sighed, "Believe me, I'll be just fine. I don't want any company right now."

Malcom stepped over to her. "I'm sorry, but this is my job. This is what I do."

Toni put her hand up in a stopping motion. "You don't hear well, do you?"

Malcom stared at her, his face void of expression. Toni marveled at how huge he was, standing there like the Rock of Gibraltar. Turning, she walked to the front entrance, but out of the corner of her eye she saw Malcom closing in on her. Abruptly she turned towards him and said stiffly, "If you want to keep your job, I suggest you go get lost elsewhere."

He stared at her. She thought she saw a plea for understanding in his eyes. At that same moment, a man appeared near Toni. "Miss, is this fellow giving you a problem?"

Toni turned to the man and was surprised to see that he stood only about five-feet-four and weighed no more than a hundred and thirty pounds. She quickly put her hand to her mouth to keep from laughing. *Oh, my goodness,* she thought.

The man arched his neck while attempting to straighten his bow tie. He looked at Malcom scornfully, then at Toni appreciatively. "If you're having a problem, I'm more than delighted to intervene."

At that, Toni wanted to laugh outright but managed to hold it in. Her insides were churning with amusement as she looked at the little man and thought of Pee-wee Herman. Then she looked at Malcom, who was standing without expression.

Bravely, the little man walked over to Malcom, cleared his throat, arched his neck, and raised his head up as if stretching towards the ceiling. "I beg your pardon, sir, but I do believe the lady is not interested in your advances."

There were several people milling around with concerned looks on their faces, naturally, for the little man. Malcom looked down at the little man, then at Toni. In the blink of an eye, he had picked up the little man by both shoulders and set him aside as if he were a useless object needing to be removed.

The little man trembled as he fought to regain his courage. His eyes were bulging with fear as he attempted to put up a charade of defiance. "Who do you think you are?" he cowered in a whisper.

Malcom looked at the little man with a grimacing look, then heard Toni say, "Malcom, please! Let him be." Malcom nodded his head as if to agree that it wasn't worth his time to deal with this little person.

The little man was still trembling as he moved cautiously away, mumbling, "You think I'm afraid of you? You'll be hearing from my attorney." Then he disappeared like a puff of smoke. Several bystanders were amused at the spectacle—until Malcom turned his attention toward them. Suddenly, one man pushed his wife ahead of him. "Move, dear, I don't want any problems."

Two security personnel arrived in the lobby and looked around suspiciously. They made eye contact with Malcom, then the one scratched his head while glancing at his counterpart. "Everything seems to be just fine here. I wonder what that little fellow was talking about." With that, they left.

Toni walked over to Malcom. "There's nothing I can do to get rid of you, right? Okay, fine. Just don't make it too obvious that you're following me." She waited for a moment to see if he would respond, but he just stood there, expressionless. As she turned to leave, Malcom let a slight smile come across his face. He flexed his muscles within his sports jacket. He had won.

chapter eleven

A Cup of Cappuccino

TONI EXITED THE FRONT DOOR and took a deep breath of cool, evening air. The night appeared calm though people were bustling about on the street. The cars, mainly the cabs, seemed quieter than usual. She noticed several couples cozily walking, arms entwined with one another. Lights shined brightly from all the nightclubs, theatres, and hotels, offering various forms of entertainment.

"Maybe you need a coat, Miss Morrison."

She turned to see Malcom standing a few feet from her. Toni welcomed the slight breeze she felt on her arms. Ignoring him, she slowly walked, looking up at the high-rises. "This feels wonderful," she mumbled as a smile crept across her face.

A car horn blew loudly. She winced at the harsh sound invading her world as a stretch limo drove by. She turned slightly to see that Malcom was only a few feet behind her, then she continued to walk down 54th Street. A display in a boutique window caught her attention. Beyond that, she observed an adult theatre with numerous people going in or coming out. *All for a cheap thrill,* she thought. Two young girls passed her giggling, obviously out for a night of adventure. One said, "Hey, big boy," and blew a kiss at Malcom. He ignored them—like everything else—if it didn't have anything to do with his job. Deep down, Toni really admired him. He was fearless, dedicated, and loyal about his position.

A calm settled on Toni that she hadn't experienced for quite a long time. It was almost as if she were totally alone. Oddly, yet comforting, for a brief moment she was far away in some distant place, some serene place. She looked up into the sky—at least the part that she could see between the tall buildings. There a star twinkled brightly. She smiled as she remembered the childlike rhyme, "Twinkle, twinkle, little star, how I wonder ..." She even felt like a child at that moment and giggled to herself.

She hadn't noticed the stretch limo cruising along beside her, keeping pace. Then suddenly Malcom pulled at her arm. She was startled out of her reverie as she looked into Malcom's intense, alert eyes. She thought she saw fear, but how could that be? Malcom wasn't afraid of anything. Was it terror?

As she tried to read him, he gripped her arm firmly. "What are you doing?" she almost yelled. Instead of answering, he pushed her in back of him. Next, he unbuttoned his jacket, cracked his knuckles, and balled up his fists. He was ready for action. By then, the limo had come to a complete stop. Malcom's face was so tense the veins in his neck were protruding. His breath was short. Toni looked at the limo as the tinted window began to ease down ever so slowly. Her heart was pounding as she stood behind Malcom, his body shielding her completely. Then a voice with a familiar French accent spoke out from the limo, "Mademoiselle Morrison."

Toni peered around Malcom's massiveness. Again the voice spoke, "Do not be alarmed! It's only I, Jean Plushette."

Toni gave a sigh of relief, then noticed Malcom was already at the limo in an attempt to snatch the door off its hinges. She yelled, "Malcom, Malcom. It's okay. I know the gentleman."

Malcom turned to her with a slight frown as if to say, "Lady, I'm just doing my job."

Toni walked over to him and gently placed her hand on his arm. "It's really okay."

He eased his hand off the door handle and looked at Toni in bewilderment. She smiled at him. "I know this gentleman."

Jean Plushette exited the limo, dressed in a tux and looking as if he was going to or coming from a queen's ball. His smile was as genuine as it had been in Toni's dressing room. His eyes sparkled with delight. Toni's heart began to pound erratically. Jean stepped over to her and reached for her hand. At that same instant, Malcom took his massive hand, placed it on Monsieur Plushette's shoulder, and squeezed it firmly. Toni spoke, "Malcom." He released his grip.

Jean rubbed his shoulder, attempting to hide the pain he felt. He looked at Malcom, somewhat smiling, and said, "My! What strong hands you have." He was attempting to be cordial.

"I'm sorry," Toni said, looking at Malcom with an air of contempt. "He didn't really mean to. He's just doing his job."

"And a fine one at that, I must say" Jean responded, looking at Toni. "My driver was taking me about when suddenly I saw you and this giant of a man following you. Naturally I became concerned, for surely, I thought, the damsel was in distress. New York is a glitzy town; however, one can never be too cautious."

Toni nodded in agreement.

Jean looked at Malcom. "Let me guess, body-guard, right?"

Malcom merely looked at him with a blank face. Jean looked at Toni, "So where are you off to, my dear?"

Toni nodded down the street. "My hotel is just a few blocks from here so I decided to walk. You know, get some fresh air."

Jean pointed down the street. "There's a small, quiet diner around the corner from your hotel. Permit me to invite you for a cup of cappuccino."

Toni was about to say no when Jean implored, "I promise you'll be home before the eagle flies."

Toni smiled, feeling unusually zesty. Malcom moved in front of Jean. "Miss Morrison wishes to be left alone."

Jean looked at Toni with somewhat pleading eyes. Toni fidgeted, looked at Malcom, and said, "It's okay. I'll be at the hotel before you know it."

With a flourish, Jean opened the limo door, and Toni eased in. Just before entering himself, Jean turned to Malcom with a coy smile and winked. Then the limo sped away. Malcom just stood watching until the limo was no longer in view.

chapter twelve ▬▬▬

Last Night Dinner

Toni and Jean sat across from each other, making small talk that didn't amount to much. She listened as he told her about his exploits venturing around the world, mostly on his yacht. She twirled her fork in the salad that sat before her somewhat distracted in thought. Jean looked at her curiously while his fingers tapped on the table. "Is there something wrong?" he asked.

Toni lazily placed the fork on the table. She stared out the window beside their table. Unexpectedly, her eyes watered at the corners. She didn't want to cry, not now, not in front of him. He reached over and took both her hands into his, but she continued staring out the window. Gently he squeezed her hands. "A penny for your thoughts," he said in a whisper.

Toni turned to face him. "I was just thinking, thinking of all the people who want to be loved, yet find no one. The world is such a cruel and strange place. So much pain, misery, and anguish. Why?"

He drew his hands away from hers and pushed his plate aside. In his deepest French accent, biting his lower lip, he replied, "I don't know why. I've never really bothered myself with the thought."

Toni looked at him surprised. "Don't you care about people? Their lives? Their struggles?"

He picked up his dinner napkin and wiped at the corner of his mouth. "Look! We live in a world where some of us make good, okay? I didn't set things in motion for them to turn out as they did. People need a perspective and need to realize whatever fate comes at them, they must deal with it."

Before he could continue, Toni interrupted. "I guess because you were born with a silver spoon in your mouth it doesn't matter about anyone else?"

He dropped his head and sighed heavily. "I didn't say that. Besides, I wasn't born with a silver spoon in my mouth either."

Toni leaned towards him. "Do you have any idea how many homeless people are right here in America? Women with children, the elderly, the downtrodden? Can you imagine how many people go hungry at night, let alone have nowhere to sleep? You have no idea, do you?"

He looked at her in astonishment. "Am I supposed to be on some kind of guilt trip? It's *my* fault because the world is cruel, as you say? Surely you can't fault me for the distress of others' fate. Everything that I have, I earned it. I paid my dues, as you Americans would say. I never asked anyone for anything. As a young man, my father told me I wouldn't amount to very much. I heard this day in and day out. It was sickening. I promised myself I would work hard, learn as I go, and keep a watchful eye. I worked, I learned, I saw successful men enjoying the fruits of their labor. I made up my mind—whatever it takes, I'm going to get there—even if it meant stepping on a few toes to do it. Why should I be responsible for someone else's failures?"

The waitress walked over to their table. "Is there anything else you folks would like to have?"

Toni stared intensely at Jean. He attempted a cordial smile at the waitress. "Thank you, I believe we're just fine."

The waitress looked at Toni and wondered about that last statement. Then she nodded at them both and walked away. Jean looked at Toni. A blank expression masked her face. She continued to stare at him. He smiled. "What?" as he looked out the window to see a couple standing nearby. They were embracing and kissing each other passionately. He turned to Toni. "Let's be sensible. You're too beautiful to be getting upset."

Toni smirked. "Oh, really now? Mr. Big Shot made it on his own. Don't owe anything to anybody. By the way, how *did* you make your fortune? By the blood and sweat of others?" She was totally surprised by the grimace on his face. Then she noticed the vein in his neck pulsating to an angry beat.

"You don't know me!" he almost yelled. He looked around to see several patrons staring at him. He smiled and nodded as he thought to himself, *No need to entertain.* Turning to Toni with a smile on his face, he said, "My dear, this is not the place or time for such a discussion. Maybe we can go elsewhere to discuss this, like your hotel suite."

Toni swallowed uncomfortably. "Look, Jean, you're a very impressionable person, handsome to say the least. However, I believe it's better that you and I should say our goodbyes for now. It is rather late, and I am awfully tired. Besides, I'm expecting someone shortly."

He looked at her coyly. "That *someone* wouldn't happen to be your lover, would it?"

Toni reached over and slapped him. "How dare you insinuate that I'm nothing more than a piece of meat!"

"I didn't mean that at all, my dear. I was only implying that whoever the gentleman was, he was very lucky. That's all I really meant. I'm sorry if I made you feel otherwise."

Toni shifted in the booth seat. She turned and saw a woman across from them giving her the thumbs-up. She felt so foolish. She thought to herself, *That wasn't lady-like at all*. She looked at Jean. He almost seemed timid, resolved to insecurity. "Look, I'm sorry. I was out of line. I had no business whatsoever to do that."

Jean smiled. "It was nothing! Coming from such a lovely creature as yourself, I would welcome it again, Mademoiselle."

They both smiled at each other. "It's getting late," Toni said as she reached for her purse.

"Then I will make sure you get to your hotel suite safely," he replied gallantly as he took out a wad of bills and placed a hundred dollar bill on the table. Then he rose and extended his hand out to her.

chapter thirteen

Good Night

TONI AND JEAN ARRIVED AT her hotel suite. As they stood in the hallway, he admired the plush carpet. "Well," Toni said, searching her purse for her key card, "thank you for the dinner."

He smiled. "It was my pleasure. Please forgive me if I made you feel uncomfortable tonight."

Toni smiled with a little uneasiness. He looked at her with sincere interest. "I would like·to see you again, beautiful lady."

Toni ran her fingers through her hair. "I don't know. I think maybe not. With my schedule and all, it's just too demanding. I'm here one moment, then I'm off elsewhere, doing what I do. I just wouldn't have the time to be sociable."

He leaned towards her and kissed her on the cheek. "Wherever you go, I will follow. My heart is telling me to not let you get far."

Awkwardly, Toni spoke, "We don't even know each other, not like that. Besides, I'm sure there are women who would love to be romanced by the likes of you."

Almost in a whisper he said, "No woman has captured my heart as you."

Toni shook her head. "We're acting like teenagers. Maybe under different circumstances we might have gone out several times. I'm not interested in one-night affairs." She gazed into his eyes and saw something that made her soul stir.

Gently he took her hand and placed it on his heart. "Neither am I."

Toni asked herself, "What is he saying? Trying to say?" she withdrew her hand from his chest, turned to the entrance door of her suite, then heard him say, "I love you, Toni." She was so taken by the words, she turned quickly to find his lips pressed up against her very own. Her mind was screaming "No" but her heart was saying "Yes." She wanted to pull away, *needed* to pull away, but no way was that going to happen at that moment. She felt her entire body rising from the floor.

Her eyes closed, fearful of opening them and revealing an illusion. Her body tingled, her breath short, her breasts heaved. Something was working its way down her inner thigh. *Oh, my goodness,* she thought. *He's not ...* She realized how deep her yearning for intimacy had become by the wetness between her legs. At last she opened her eyes to find she was alone. He had gone. She looked to the left, then to the right, only to find that she stood alone in the hallway. She sighed as she leaned against the door. *How long has it been?* she thought.

Opening the door to go in, she whispered, "Too long." With that, she fell lazily on the bed, looking up at the ceiling. Even though she felt tired, she was invigorated at the thought of Jean. "What is it about this man?" her mind almost screamed out. She was curious and wanted to know, yet there was the tension of restraint, knowing deep within there was a pitfall.

As the ceiling swirled around and around, she abruptly sat up. "I need a warm shower" she spoke as if someone else was in the room besides herself. She began to undress, feeling the tension across her back. Stepping into the shower, Toni thought she had turned the water to lukewarm, but she mistakenly turned on the cold. As the cold beads pelted her body, she almost screamed.

She quickly adjusted the dial and luxuriated in the warmth that cascaded down upon her. Sponging herself gently with her eyes closed, Toni imagined that she was on a tropical island, standing beneath a waterfall. She felt her nipples on her breast harden. She arched her back as the lather of soap lay in patches about her body. A tingling went through her body like a mild electric shock. She was suddenly torn from her tropical fantasy by the ringing of the phone.

She paused for a moment, thinking, "Who could that be?" Stepping out of the shower, she wrapped a towel around herself and walked to the phone. At first she hesitated, staring at it for a moment. As the phone continued to ring, she finally picked it up and said, "Hello?"

The voice on the other end was familiar. "Toni, sweetheart! Are you okay? I see you made it. Good girl."

Toni sighed. "Liz, I should have known. Who else would be calling this late?"

Toni heard Liz chuckle. "Sweetheart, everyone was expecting you. They were so disappointed. Of course, I had them understand you were tired and had a slight headache. Oh, by the way, I met a Mr. Rubenstein from Golden Republic Studio. It's located somewhere out in California. He wanted to know if you would be interested in a part in a movie that he is considering doing. Of course, I told him that you would be delighted. Isn't that wonderful? He feels that the part is made undeniably just for you.

"Oh, yes, we have an engagement in Munich, Germany, in a couple of months. And The Women's League of Breast Cancer Awareness wants you to speak at their annual conference next month. I almost forgot—Oprah's producers want to know when you can make an appearance. Isn't this all wonderful?"

Toni didn't say anything. She just held the receiver.

"Toni? Toni, are you there sweetheart?"

Toni drew in a breath, "Yes, Liz, I'm here."

Again Liz continued, "We've got to get some new clothes for you."

Toni sighed, "Liz, I'm sitting here with a towel wrapped around me. Can we talk in the morning over breakfast? I really want to sleep."

Liz chuckled, "Of course, sweetheart, I'm sorry. By the way, did Malcom do his job?"

Toni looked to the ceiling and shook her head, "Yes, Liz, Malcom did his job."

Liz attempted to continue in conversation. "You know, sweetheart—"

But Toni cut her off with "Good night, Liz," and hung up the phone.

chapter fourteen

An Encounter over Coffee

TONI AWAKENED FEELING REFRESHED. SHE rolled over to look at the alarm clock on the dresser. It was 8 a.m. She thought to herself, *I was sure it was later than that. Oh, what a good night's sleep will do for a body.* Lazily she sat up in bed, stretched her arms overhead, and rotated her head from side to side. She felt good. She slowly eased from the bed and walked over to the window to pull the drapes back. The sunlight gave way to sudden brightness that caused Toni to immediately close the drapes. Sauntering over to the dresser, she turned on the clock radio.

"Oh, what a beautiful morning it is here in the Big Apple. It's going to be a fantastic day," she heard the announcer say.

For a moment, she considered having breakfast in bed, but said "Naw." The clock showed 8:15. She knew that Liz was probably still counting sheep. She didn't really want to wake her simply for breakfast, so she washed her face, brushed her teeth, put her hair in a ponytail, slipped into a pair of blue jeans and a sweatshirt, threw on some comfortable sneakers, and headed out the door. Arriving at the elevator, she pushed the down button and waited patiently for the elevator to arrive.

The hotel dining area had only a few people scattered at various tables. Some of the people appeared to have been up all night, and were now seeking a good hot cup of coffee in hopes that it would help them to jump start their day.

One gentleman appeared to be so tired, he was barely able to hold onto the paper he was attempting to read. Toni's mind drifted for a moment to the hallway scene between her and Jean. "It was just a dream," she mumbled to herself.

"Good morning, Ma'am! Would you like a menu?"

Toni looked up to see a smiling waiter standing at her table.

"Anything special this morning, Ma'am?"

Before Toni answered him, she tilted her head back, breathing in the pleasing aroma of freshly brewed coffee. "May I get several slices of rye toast with some marmalade and a cup of that wonderful smelling coffee?"

The waiter bowed gracefully at her. "Would there be anything else, Ma'am?"

Toni politely shook her head. "That will be all for now, thank you."

"Thank you, Ma'am," the waiter said as he backed away and bumped into a table that was behind him. He turned so swiftly, one would have assumed that he was being attacked by an unseen deity. Then he headed toward the kitchen area almost at a gallop. Toni smiled as she fidgeted with the napkin on the table.

She happened to turn to her right, where she observed a man looking at her in a unusual and strange manner. Toni tried to avoid eye contact with him. His stare was cold and penetrating. He seemed out of place in the restaurant. Toni thought that he belonged elsewhere. Nervously, she fumbled with the napkin on the table. As if coming to her rescue, the waiter arrived with her rye toast and a pot of hot coffee. He placed them before her and smiled. "Is there anything else that I can get for you, Ma'am?"

Toni assured him that everything was fine. As he turned to leave, the waiter appeared to bump into the stranger, then oddly, continued toward the kitchen without saying a word. The man stood, walked over to Toni's table, and paused. He looked down at her. Toni refused to acknowledge his presence. She looked into her reflection in the coffee cup, inhaling its rich aroma. The man grunted, obviously trying to get Toni's attention. She continued to stare into the cup of coffee. She felt like small needles were pricking her on the neck. She didn't know this man. *Why is he trying to get close to me?* she thought.

"Pardon me," he stated.

Toni looked about casually, as if attempting to identify where the sound had come from. Knowing that the man was standing near her, she awkwardly pretended to be startled as she met his penetrating eyes.

"Oh, my! I didn't even realize someone was standing there."

The man looked at her intensely. He moved to seat himself across from her. Leaning towards her, his eyes fixed directly on hers, he warned, "Be very careful! The devil goes about like a roaring lion, seeking whom it can destroy. Resist evil." That message delivered, the man rose from the table and walked away as if he had never been there at all.

Toni sat with her mouth dropped open, completely startled at what just took place. She turned in the direction that the man had gone, but there was no one there. She looked at the table where the man had previously sat, but it, too, was empty. Her mind was racing, thought after thought. She was trying to make sense of all of it, but it would not come together.

"Is everything okay?" she heard the waiter ask.

Toni turned to him. "Can you tell me about that gentleman who was sitting there at that table?"

The waiter turned in the direction that Toni was pointing. "That table there?" he asked, pointing in the same area that Toni was pointing.

"Yes," Toni replied. "Who was the man that was sitting there?"

The waiter raised his brow and looked somewhat confused. "I didn't see anyone sitting over there."

"You had to," Toni almost screamed. "You bumped into him here at my table."

"I'm sorry, Ma'am, but there was no one there."

Toni nodded, "Sure, thanks!"

chapter fifteen

Strange People in New York

Toni hadn't realized that Liz had entered the dining area. Standing at the entrance, she scanned the room before spotting Toni. As she approached, she gleefully exclaimed, "Oh, here you are, darling!"

Toni sipped her coffee while Liz seated herself after placing her purse in the empty chair at their table. She sighed heavily. "Last night was a doozy. I didn't realize how much champagne I had consumed."

Toni sipped her coffee while studying Liz. "Uh-uh."

Liz smiled as she picked up the menu. "And a good morning to you, too. So, what are we having this morning? Got to put some fuel in the tank. We got a long day ahead of us."

The waiter arrived at the table. His gaze was fixed on Toni as he spoke to Liz. "Would you like to order, Ma'am?"

Liz looked at Toni, who was smiling, then back at the waiter. "You talking to me or to her?" Liz asked defiantly.

The waiter didn't bat an eye as he continued his visual assault on Toni. Without looking at Liz, he pointed his finger at her. "I'm talking to you."

Liz drew in a deep breath. "I suggest you face me when asking a question. It's rude and impolite and definitely nonengaging otherwise."

Toni reached over and tapped Liz on the hand. "Liz, you're gonna lose your food before you even get it. It's okay."

Toni looked at the waiter, "Can you take her order, please?"

The waiter nodded, "Yes, Ma'am! What would you like to have?"

Toni laughed. "Not me! Her," pointing to Liz.

Tensely, he turned to Liz. "Are you ready to order?"

Liz looked at him up and down and thought to herself, *This poor excuse of something is nothing but a weasel. Who the hell does he think he is? I pay his wages.*

Her brows puckered in fury as her lower lip quivered. She looked at Toni and knew Toni was reading her. Faking a smile at the waiter, she replied, "I think I'll start with a cold glass of orange juice, a boiled egg, and two slices of wheat toast."

"Would there be anything else?" he asked, turning back to Toni.

Liz rapped the table sharply with her knuckles. "Get your ass back there and start earning your keep!"

The waiter quickly left. Toni shook her head. Liz asked, "What?"

Toni looked at her for a long moment. "Liz, why do you have to be so hard at times?"

Liz wiped at the corner of her eye. "Did you see how he ignored me? The little rodent." She sighed. "Anyway, my dear, I met some pretty fascinating people last night. Several have a special interest in wanting to see you further your career. Isn't that just wonderful?" she gushed.

Toni knew if money were involved, Liz would have her hand in it by some means or other.

The waiter placed the boiled egg, toast, and orange juice in front of Liz. "I hope it's to your liking, Ma'am."

Liz stared at him, thinking, *You little rodent.* Instead, she smiled. "Thank you, I believe this will be just fine for now," as she buttered a slice of toast. The waiter did not move.

Toni said, "We're fine, thank you."

He left, going to other tables as the room began to become more active with patrons. Liz cracked the egg shell and looked over at Toni, who seemed to be lost in a fog. "Are you alright, dear?" Liz asked as she continued to watch Toni.

Toni looked at Liz intently. "There was a strange man here, sitting over there at that table."

Liz turned in the direction that Toni was nodding towards. "I don't see anybody over there," Liz whispered as she turned back to her provisions that sat before her.

Toni swallowed and thought, *Liz, you can really be a bimbo at times.* But she said, "He's not here now; he's gone. He was watching me—*staring* at me."

Liz smiled. "Sweetheart, *everyone* watches you. You're a jewel. A rare one at that. If I had twenty dollars for every man that looked at you, I could retire ever so happily. I may have gotten my order taken more quickly if that little rodent of a waiter hadn't been staring at you for so long."

Toni looked around then leaned over the table towards Liz. "Really, Liz, this guy gave me the chills."

Liz took a bite of her toast. "Whoa! Chills, huh? I wouldn't mind some guy giving me chills right about now. I haven't had a good lay in a good while. I *need* some chills."

Toni whispered somewhat annoyingly, "Liz, I'm serious. Listen to me. This guy came and stood by my table—this table right here. First, he didn't say anything. He just kept staring at me. His eyes were cold—penetrating."

Liz smiled, "Oh, I like him already. Did he leave a number?"

Toni hit the table furiously. "Liz, I'm not playing. This is no game. Will you listen to me?"

Liz looked at the table. "Toni, you've spilled half of my juice. What gives?"

Toni apologized. "I'm sorry. You want another glass or bottle?"

They both looked at each other and started to laugh. Liz took a small bite of her egg. "Okay! What's the deal with this strange guy?"

Again, Toni looked around the restaurant, struggling to find the right words. "Liz, this guy seats himself across from me and says without any expression or emotion, 'Beware of him that seeketh to destroy.'"

Toni looked at Liz, waiting for a response. Liz looked at Toni, waiting for her to continue. "Well?" Toni said.

"Well, what?" Liz replied.

Toni folded her hands and put them in her lap. "You haven't heard a word I've said, have you?"

Liz brushed away the few crumbs that fell from the slice of toast she was about to bite into. "Of course, I heard what you said. I was just wondering, why would he say something like that to you?"

"That's what I don't understand, Liz. I'm left in a stupor. Suddenly, I feel so vulnerable. Is it worth contacting the police?"

Liz shrugged. "What're you gonna tell them? A strange man came up to you and said, 'Beware, one comes to destroy'?"

Toni nodded. "You're right. They might think that something's wrong with me. After all, on any given day, you can find strange people in New York."

chapter sixteen

A Heart-to-Heart Talk

As THE TWO WOMEN ENTERED Toni's suite, the phone rang. Toni paused and stared at it.

"Aren't you going to answer?" Liz asked curiously as she looked at Toni.

Toni didn't move. Her gaze lay fixed on the phone. Liz walked over and picked up the receiver. "Hello? Hello! Is anyone there?" the dial tone buzzed. She hung up the receiver. "Apparently, whoever it was didn't want to speak to me. Someone I don't know about?"

Toni shook her head. "I have no idea who that may have been."

Liz plopped down in the well-padded Easy-chair as Toni sat before the mirrored vanity. "Liz, what do you think he meant when he said, 'Beware of him that seeketh to destroy'?"

Liz shrugged her shoulders. "He probably was a crackpot. Saw your picture somewhere, recognized you in the restaurant, felt the need to approach you, so he did by saying something stupid."

Toni studied herself in the mirror. "It just doesn't make sense. It's really weird."

"It wouldn't happen to have anything to do with last night, would it?"

Toni looked at Liz in a quizzical way. "Last night? What happened last night?"

Liz rose from the chair and straightened her clothes, attempting to focus on the situation at hand. She paused in front of Toni, took her face in the palms of her hands, and asked, "Who is he, Toni?"

"Who is who? Liz, what are you talking about?"

Liz walked toward the entrance door of the suite, then suddenly turned and placed her hands on her hips. "The guy you had a late-night dinner with. The guy that stood right outside of *this* door last night."

Toni stood up and walked directly to Liz. "You know about that?"

Liz walked to the patio balcony and back again. "Sweetheart, there isn't very much that I don't know about, at least when it comes to you. Toni, I've been here since your first successful modeling stunt. Remember, dear, I'm the other mommie."

Toni walked right up to Liz and looked her directly in the eyes. "No more, Liz, no more charades. I want you to stay out of my personal life. I realize your concern for me. However, you have to understand—I need room—I need air—I need to be alone when I feel like I want to be alone—I need someone or something in my life that will appreciate me for just being me. I'm tired of being Miss Morrison this, Miss Morrison that. I'm tired of you watching every move that I make. I'm tired of you hanging on to me. I'm tired of you telling me how much I remind you of yourself when you were younger. I'm tired of you trying to be a mother, when I have my own. I'm just plain sick and tired of it all. I'm tired of people telling me how beautiful I am. I'm tired of men looking at me with lust. I'm tired of women giving me fake smiles, then behind my back, tear me down."

Toni paused for a breath. She hadn't realized how long she had ranted on until she saw the tears streaming down her friend's face. Toni pressed both of her hands to her head. "Oh, my God, what have I done? I didn't mean that. I really didn't. I'm awfully sorry, Liz. I don't know what came over me."

Liz stared at Toni with the tears continuing to flow. "All I ever tried to do was be there for you. Yes, it's partially true. I live my life over by seeing myself in you. But I grew to love you as if you were my own daughter. I'm not so foolish to believe that I could ever give you the love that your own mom gives you. My ultimate concern is to protect you from the sharks as much as I know how. I've seen how they play the game, darling. They'll make you, then they'll break you. Strip you of everything—throw you to the wolves—make you feign for yourself. Make the most of it while you can, get paid, stash it away, invest it, then when that time arrives, you can hold your head up high and walk out with your dignity. Sweetheart, I would never hurt you in anyway."

Toni extended her arms out to Liz. They both embraced and cried on each other's shoulder. Toni sobbed, "I'm tired, Liz, and I'm afraid. Success has become more than I can bear!"

Liz firmly placed her hands on Toni's shoulders and looked her in the eyes. "Sweetheart, you've earned this. This is your time. You've paid your dues. You're a successful fashion model and loved by the world."

"And," she giggled, "more by men than anyone else."

Toni walked to the patio balcony and pulled the drapes back to expose the sunlight. She stared at the skyscrapers, then turned to Liz. "You never mention how you feel about my parents—meaning that my father is white and my mom is black. So what does that make me—a mutt?"

Liz looked alarmed, "How dare you! Who cares if your father's a German shepherd and your mom's a collie? Look what they produced! A fine cocker spaniel. Honey, you're beautiful—not just on the outside. You've got a beautiful heart. That's what really counts. When I came to America as a young girl, I had all sorts of dreams. As I entered into the modeling phase of my career, I often wondered if I would be totally accepted because of me being German. Well, my career went pretty well. No one seemed to care that I was what I was. But, of course, when the aging process began to be more visible, well, it became time to start thinking about other avenues. Look! Why don't you tidy up? I'm going to my room for a sec, then we'll meet in the lobby, take a cab, go shopping, and do a little sight-seeing."

Liz kissed Toni on the forehead and left.

chapter seventeen ▬
A Shopping Trip

TONI PICKED UP HER PURSE and jacket and started towards the door. Suddenly the phone rang. She smiled, thinking that Liz was calling to be sure that she had left. She picked the receiver up. "Hello?" There was a short moment of silence on the other end, when suddenly, the all too-familiar French accent sounded.

"Good morning, you lovely creature. How are you this morning?"

Surprised, Toni asked, "How did you get this number?"

Jean sighed at the other end of the receiver. "My dear, you're staying at a hotel."

Toni replied, "This number wasn't supposed to be given out to anyone without my approval."

He laughed. "My dear, this is New York. If the dollar is right, one can get anything one wants."

Toni almost stuttered. "What do you want?"

Jean, smiling on the other end, said, "Of course, I want *you*, Toni. Toni, my lovely Toni, why don't we get together this evening? I promise to make it a fun-filled evening, something you'll never forget."

She shrugged. "I'm sorry, but I do have another engagement."

Jean replied, "I'm sure Liz wouldn't mind."

Toni was startled. "How do you know Liz? Has she spoken to you?"

"No, my dear, but I have my sources. She appears to be a very loyal confident. Toni, I really wish to see you. There's something that I want to share with you."

Toni was hesitant. "I don't know. Maybe when I come back we can talk. What's your number? I'll call."

There was a pause. "I'll call you, my dear." The phone went dead. Toni looked at the receiver, then hung up. Something inside of her was emerging. She felt somewhat excited and at the same time, fearful. This man, Jean, how was it he was drawing her to him? Toni thought, *I don't even really know him.* Yet, there was yearning, a stirring inside of her creating desire within her. She got goose bumps just thinking about it.

The phone rang again. Toni immediately picked it up. "I told you I have something to do!"

Liz said, "I thought we were going shopping."

Toni nervously laughed. "I'm just kidding. I'll be right down." She hung up the receiver and left the suite. When she stepped off the elevator into the lobby, she heard Liz say to some woman, "I'll talk to you later."

"Who was that?" Toni asked.

"Uh, that was Rebecca Shepard. She's the editor for a new glamour magazine. She's interested in doing a piece on clothing styles for today's fashion models. Well, my dear, you look all ready to splurge. I like those jeans you're wearing. They fit you perfectly. Let's grab a cab out front."

After a day of shopping and sight-seeing, Liz and Toni were ready to get back to the hotel and relax. As the cab pulled up to the front entrance of the hotel, Liz complained impatiently, "Damn, my feet are killing me. I want to sit in a hot tub of bubbly and maybe have a glass of white wine and slowly slip into oblivion. How're you feeling, dear?"

Toni shrugged. "OK, I guess. Just a little tired."

The cab driver quickly opened the doors for both of them. They emerged with bags in both hands. "Miss Morrison?" Toni heard someone say.

She looked to see a photographer focusing his camera at her for a shoot. Toni let several bags fall to the curb while she struggled to put her sunglasses on. Liz yelled, "Go get a life! Can't you see we want a little privacy?"

The photographer continued snapping pictures. The doorman almost tripped in his attempt to help Toni with her bags. Toni shielded one side of her face with her hand as she scurried into the hotel lobby. Waiting at the elevator, she noticed a man with his back toward her. He suddenly turned, smiled, and nodded at her.

"It's him! That's the guy!" Toni mumbled to herself. She looked for Liz, who was giving the photographer a piece of her mind. When she turned to the area where the man had been standing, he was gone. She looked about frantically, but he was nowhere to be seen. She stood there, shaking her head, reflecting back to her earlier encounter with him. *Who is he? Is he telling me something? Is he trying to warn me about someone? Who sent him? Why me?*

Liz finally arrived at the elevator, struggling with the bags. She looked at one of the bell-hops as if to say, "You kosher-head. Can't you see I need help?" Then she looked at Toni and said, "Damn people just get on my nerves."

The elevator doors opened. They stepped in and proceeded to their suites. Once arriving at their floor, Liz exited, dragging several bags. She called out to Toni, "I'll see you in a bit, sweetheart. I've really got to rest my feet."

Before entering her suite, Toni looked up and down the hallway. She wasn't expecting anything, but she wanted to be sure.

chapter eighteen

Back in Touch with Loved Ones

TONI CASUALLY LET HER BAGS drop to the floor. At the moment, she wasn't interested in any of the items she had purchased. Suddenly, she thought she heard someone talking just outside her door, but looking through the peephole, she saw no one. Tired, she walked to the bedroom and lay across the bed. Her mind raced, thinking of the man she saw in the lobby. Perplexed, she asked herself, "What is this all about?" Then she got up and went to the phone. "I need to call Mom and Dad."

She dialed and waited. After several rings, she hung up the receiver. It was only 5:30 in New York, so that would make it be 2:30 Pacific time. Browsing through her personal phone book, she noticed Norma's number. She wondered how her old childhood friend was doing. They hadn't seen each other for a while. Once again, she attempted to call her parents. The phone rang and on the third ring, she heard the all too-familiar voice of a loved one.

"Hello?"

"Mom, is it really you?"

On the other end of the phone, her mother almost screamed. "Toni, baby, how are you? Your dad and I were just wondering about you. Oh, baby, it's so good to hear from you. Is everything OK? You haven't called in days, so we began to worry. Are you still in New York? How did the fashion show go?"

Toni was smiling. "Mom, I'm fine. The show was terrific. New York is New York—big and kind of scary."

"What do you mean 'kind of scary'?"

"Ah, Mom, it's just a big place with lots of people, some stranger than others, I guess. How's Dad? Is he there?"

"Yes, he's standing right next to me. He heard me say your name and sprung from his chair like a jack-in-the-box. Hold on for a second."

"Toni, how you doing, kiddie-o?"

Toni smiled. She felt really alive after hearing her father's voice. "Hi, Dad, how are you doing? I miss you and Mom so much. As you know, I've been quite busy. This modeling can take its toll if people don't set priorities."

Lester Morrison agreed. "Baby, why don't you come home and relax for a while? Your mom and I would really enjoy the company."

Tears gathered in Toni's eyes. "I know, Dad, I would love to, but I must finish these other modeling assignments. I'm under contract. After I've finished, we'll all take a vacation. Maybe go to Hawaii or Canada. How does that sound?"

Lester turned to his wife, "She said we can all go to Hawaii for a vacation when she's through with her assignments."

Gina Morrison nodded in agreement. "That sounds wonderful."

Lester spoke into the receiver, "Toni, Mom said that's great. Is it cold back there?"

Toni was shaking her head, "No, not really. Just kind of mild."

"Where's Liz?" he asked.

"Oh, she's in her suite, probably taking a nap."

"Tell her we love her and hope to see you both soon. I love you, kiddie-o."

"I love you too, Dad. Tell Mom when I come home, I'll be looking forward to that tuna casserole. Give her a kiss for me. I got to go for now, but I'll be in touch. Take care of yourselves. By the way, if you happen to see Norma, tell her I haven't forgotten her. She's still my sister, and I love her. Bye, Dad."

Toni hung up the receiver, then sat for a moment, tears streaming down her face. *I love them so much.*

chapter nineteen—
Dinner Plans

THE PHONE RANG. TONI PICKED it up. "Yes?"

"Hey, you wanna go out to dinner?" Liz asked.

"Where did you have in mind?" Toni questioned.

"I hear that new restaurant, 'Key Largo,' is supposed to be fantastic. It's quite upper class and has a clientele to match. Who knows, we might get lucky. Of course, *you* wouldn't need any luck. If you were a turd, flies would be waiting in line to get to you." Liz laughed hysterically.

"I don't know, Liz."

"Shit, we got to eat," Liz roared.

Toni thought to herself, *How can she say some of the things that come out of her mouth?*

"Well, sweetheart, shall we have a go at it?" Liz asked again.

Toni didn't want to answer right away, so she said, "Just before you called, I spoke with Mom and Dad. They sent you their love. I don't know why," Toni laughed.

"Funny, very funny, Toni. How are they anyway?"

Toni replied, "Oh, they're just fine. Want me to come home. Liz, after these modeling sessions, why don't we all take a vacation somewhere? Maybe Hawaii or Canada."

"Hawaii or Canada? Are you kidding? *Nobody* goes to those places anymore. That's like going to Disneyland. You go one time, that's more than enough. It's not romantic like it used to be. It's a resort for old, retired people. Honey, I still got a spring or two left in the old cahoot. I want adventure, some teasing."

Toni asked, "Liz, I don't mean to be personal, but why didn't your marriage work out?"

There was a pause. "Marriage! I really never knew the meaning of the word. I was young, and, of course, beautiful, at least that's what I was led to believe. My modeling career was blooming, and it looked as if I was going places. Then I met *him*. I'm speaking of Curt, of course. Oh, girl, if you could have seen this man. He was everything I could hope for—yearned for. Yesss! My knight in shining armor. I was swept off my feet just by his presence alone.

To make a long story short, we went to dinner one night. A candlelit dinner, matter of fact, at Picasso's Restaurant. He sat across the table from me and smiled such a smile, I literally wet my panties. I thought, what magic does this man have to make me react this way?

I remember the waiter coming to our table with a bottle of champagne. Carl filled both our glasses, raised his at the center of the table, and toasted me. I'll never forget the words he spoke. "This is to the most beautiful, unique creation on this side of heaven. To you, my dear, I surrender my very soul."

"Girl, at that point, I almost saturated my underwear."

"Wow!" Toni said, finding it very amusing. "What happen after that?"

"Well," Liz sighed, "we went to his place, you get the picture?"

"And?" Toni exclaimed, waiting for her to continue.

"After dating each other for several months, he proposed. Yes! Asked me to marry him. I was shocked! But how could I say no? I loved this man. At least that's what I believed then. Eventually we got married. The strange thing was that I lived in our house in Newport Beach, but he lived in Bel-Air. He said it was convenient because of his work. He claimed he was a motion picture producer of sorts.

Shit! I never heard of him producing a damn thing. Anyway, come to find out, the bastard was staying with his *other* wife."

"Wow! That's really deep."

"Anyway," Liz continued, "I hired a hit man to take him out."

"You *what*?" Toni almost screamed.

Liz began laughing uncontrollably. "I'm just kidding. Got you kiddie-o. Hey, enough of the past. Are we going to dinner or what?"

"OK. Can you be ready in an hour?" Toni asked.

"Honey, I put the 'H' in hour. I'll see you shortly."

chapter twenty──
The Key Largo

TONI AND LIZ ARRIVED AT the restaurant. They were seated almost immediately in a cozy booth not far from where a young man was playing the piano. The restaurant was upscale and appeared to have a diverse clientele. Women were dressed fashionably and were draped with expensive jewels, while some of the men were in tuxes or wore name-brand suits. As Toni and Liz looked around, they noticed various smiling faces looking towards them. Men smiled and nodded, while several women sheepishly attempted to hide their contempt behind a cordial smile. The mood throughout the restaurant was light with banter.

Liz giggled, "Isn't this wonderful? Oh, my goodness, I feel like I'm among a million bucks."

As Toni looked toward the pianist, she marveled, "This is very nice."

"You look like a queen," Liz remarked. "That dress brings something out of you that's simply exquisite."

Toni smiled and leaned towards Liz, "You don't look so bad yourself."

Liz pinched her hand, and the waiter arrived at their table. "Would you ladies like to enjoy a beverage before ordering? Perhaps a glass of wine?" He provided them with a drink menu and stood with pen and pad at the ready.

"I'll have a glass of white wine, please," Toni said to the waiter, who was smiling broadly.

He looked at Liz, "And for you, Madam?"

Liz was attempting to keep a straight face, knowing what she was about to say. "Bring me a couple of cold beers."

Toni turned to her, "Liz!"

Liz patted Toni's hand. "I'm just kidding. I'll have a glass of wine as well."

The waiter nodded, "Very well. I will have it shortly."

The lights were somewhat dim, offering a romantic overtone. Toni smiled as she listened to the pianist sing, "With these hands, I'll provide for you long after the sun has lost its glow. Should there be a stormy sea, I'll turn the tide for you."

Liz whispered, "That's a beautiful song."

"Yes, it is" Toni whispered back.

The waiter returned with two wine glasses and poured the contents of the bottle into the first glass. He filled the glass halfway, looked at Toni as if to get her approval to continue, and she said, "That's fine, thank you."

He then glanced at Liz, who returned his look and challenged, "What?" The waiter held up the bottle. Liz said, "Just leave it." Carefully he placed it on the table, took a gentlemanly bow, backed away, and left.

Toni rolled her eyes at her companion. "Liz——" but before Toni could finish, Liz interrupted. "I know, I know. I promise I'll be ladylike. Have you thought about what you would like to eat?"

Toni mused, "Not really. Let's wait till we get the menu. I wonder if they got crab cakes?"

"Crab cakes?! Toni, this is an upscale restaurant. You're not down in the bayou, you know."

Toni laughed. "I know, I was just wondering."

The waiter brought the menus and handed an opened one to each of them. "Take your time, ladies," he said. "I'll be back shortly."

Liz mumbled, "He better not be gone too long. I'm hungry as hell." She didn't dare look at Toni, knowing Toni was staring at her disapprovingly.

"Ah, let's see what we have here," Liz mused.

Toni said, "I'm going to have a salad."

Liz looked at her in astonishment. "A salad? Toni, this is a restaurant. You order food here. This is not while on the run, get-what-you-can kind of thing."

Toni closed the menu. "You know I have to watch my weight."

Liz put her hand to her forehead. "Toni, your weight is fine. A little beef is not going to hurt you, believe me."

Toni shrugged, "In fact, I think I'll have the salmon salad."

"Whatever," Liz said sourly, hoping Toni didn't detect a bit of hostility toward her. I'm going to have the biggest steak they got. If it's not big enough, I'll tell 'em go find a cow and kill it."

The waiter reappeared. "Are you ladies ready to order?"

Toni gave her order. Liz still mused over the menu. "What's the largest steak you have?" she asked.

The waiter pointed to a location on the menu.

"I'll have that with some scallops, a slice of garlic bread, and some grilled onions."

The waiter nodded, retrieved the menus, and left. Toni looked at Liz. "You're going to eat *all* that?"

Liz scratched at her chin, "Of course. Why not? My modeling days are long over."

Toni excused herself to go to the ladies' room. Upon entering, she could hear the chatter among several women. The ladies' room was partitioned so that people couldn't see each other unless they were standing along side one another.

Not knowing that Toni had entered, a woman spoke in hushed tones. "She's quite beautiful. But did you know that she's a half-breed?"

Another of the women gasped. "Surely you don't mean—" but she was interrupted by the first speaker.

"I hear her mother's black and her father's white. Unbelievable, isn't it?"

Another woman chided in, "It's not unusual to find mixed couples nowadays. It's happening every-where. In spite of that, however, she *is* a beautiful creature. Did you see how the men marveled at her when she walked into the restaurant?"

One woman who was putting on lipstick spoke with bitter conviction, "If I *ever* saw my husband looking at the likes of someone like that—" At that very, moment Toni chose to make her appearance. The women's mouths dropped in shock. The one speaking attempted to counter with, "Oh, there she is. Pretty as a picture."

Toni slowly walked to the door exit near them, turned with a smile on her face, and asked, "Are any of you sure where *your* husbands were last night? If they weren't with you by bedtime, they may already have been in bed—with someone else. Good eve-ning, ladies."

With cool composure, Toni walked out. She came straight to the table where Liz was sitting and said, "I think it's time for us to go."

Liz's eyes opened wide. "Go?! I haven't even eaten yet."

chapter twenty-one

A Ruined Evening

IT WAS A LITTLE AFTER 8 in the evening when Toni and Liz arrived back at the hotel. Liz cursed all the way back, mainly at the cab driver who was trying to figure out if she was drunk or just an out-of-control bitch. Toni's head was throbbing. It felt like it was caught between two vices. Once parked at the hotel entrance, Toni jumped out of the cab and entered the lobby area, where she found a seat, sat, and buried her head in between her hands. Liz stood over her, cackling, waving her hand around in the air.

"What in the hell is your problem?" she angrily shouted at Toni. "We can't even go out for a nice dinner without you getting all emotionally disturbed because some old windbag hurt your feelings. Toni, you are what you are. You had no choice in selecting who you are. Don't you realize that you have the *best* of two worlds? Who gives a rat's ass about you being part black and white? Why do you let ignorant people unnerve you? I had to leave a perfectly good steak—not to mention the garlic bread. The evening was fine, just fine—until you got your little feelings hurt and that just made you feel the heck with everything else."

Toni stood up and without looking at Liz, walked to the elevator. "I'm going up. I have a splitting headache."

Liz stood there with her hands on her hip. "That's right! Go on to your room. Crawl in your bed and sob. I'm going to a bar, get drunk, and maybe even get lucky." She turned on her heels and walked out of the hotel.

The desk clerk walked over to Toni. "Are you alright, Ms. Morrison? Is there anything you want or need sent to your room?"

As the elevator doors opened, Toni turned to him and said, "Send a bottle of brandy to my suite."

The desk clerk looked surprised as the elevator doors closed. Toni was angry. After she entered her suite, she threw her purse across the room, took off her high heels and slung them at the TV, then she pulled at the diamond-studded earrings, almost tearing her earlobes. Finally, she plopped down on the sofa and pulled the straps of her gown down, letting them hang loosely. She thought to herself, *I'm so sick and tired of this crap.*

A knock on the door interrupted her thoughts. Toni yelled, "I'm not in the mood for your bull, Liz. Go to your suite, order yourself a big juicy steak, get full, and take your ass to bed!" In shock, Toni put her hand over her mouth. "Did I just say that?"

The knock on the door continued. She got up and looked through the peephole. It was a bellboy. Feeling defeated, she opened the door. "Ms. Morrison, here's your bottle of brandy. Would you like anything else?" he asked timidly.

Toni took the bottle and told him to wait while she went and got a five dollar bill from her purse and handed it to him. "Thank you," she said and closed the door. Then she looked at the bottle of alcohol in her hand and studied it. "I don't need this," she murmured to herself. But then, the way she was feeling, surely one little drink wouldn't hurt.

She went into the kitchen, got a glass, and poured some of the contents into it. After sipping some, she frowned at the very taste of it. "My goodness, this stuff is potent," she said, swallowing hard.

"Maybe this will help dilute it," she said to herself, walking over to the frig and pressing the ice dispenser, watching as several cubes of ice fell into the drink. Then she poured some more brandy in the glass, set the bottle on the counter, and walked back into the living room, where she picked up the TV remote and turned on the television. She settled into an awkward position on the sofa and surfed the channels until she came across a reality show.

Gradually, the alcohol began to make her feel warm, which prompted her to get up and undress down to only her bra and panties. More comfortable, she settled back down on the sofa, directing her attention once again to the TV. Her toes wiggled as she stretched out her long, shapely legs. She was beginning to relax. The tension appeared to subside. After an hour of trying to focus on the TV, her eyes closed and she surrendered to the sleep that overcame her.

Toni was sure that only a few moments had passed before she was awakened by a knock at the door. But when she looked at the clock, she saw that several hours had passed. She felt a sudden chill and realized she was only wearing her bra and panties. When she got up, she almost fell backwards and had to balance herself on the arm of the sofa. Slowly regaining her balance, she went to the bedroom and put on a robe. The brandy had relaxed her, but she was left with a mild headache. The knocking continued.

"Just a minute," she said under her breath. She knew for sure it was Liz. But when she looked through the peephole, she only saw a bouquet of flowers. Her view was obstructed. *Who would be sending flowers this late?*

"Yes? Can I help you?" she asked.

chapter twenty-two

A Late Night Visitor

Toni opened the door. To her surprise, there he stood—Jean Plushette, the Frenchman. He extended the flowers toward her. "For a lovely lady."

Toni was at a loss for words, not because of the flowers, not because of him, but because she imagined what she must look like. She finally managed to say, "What are you doing here? Do you know how late it is? This is not the time."

He smiled, "When is the time?"

She noticed he had one hand behind his back.

"What? Another surprise?"

He produced a bottle of champagne. Just then, an elderly couple passed them in the hallway. They were dressed as if they had been to an opera or the theatre. They smiled at Toni. She felt embarrassed as she closed the top of her robe.

Jean asked, "Are we going to stand out here all night, or are you going to invite me in?"

Toni pleaded, "It's awfully late. I promise I'll see you tomorrow."

"My dear, tomorrow may never come."

Toni sighed. "Look, you can come in for a few minutes, but no more than that. I have a busy schedule ahead of me." With that, she stepped back and allowed him to enter.

He looked around upon entering and said, "Nice! Very nice."

"Have a seat." She pointed him to the sofa then laid the flowers on the dining table. "What's so important that you had to come this late?"

He crossed his legs and folded his arms. "Toni, I want to share something with you," he said seriously.

"Really?" she said as she seated herself at the dining table.

He extended his hand out towards the opposite end of the sofa. "Please, sit here. I'm not accustomed to speaking across the room."

Toni got up and her robe slipped open, revealing her bra and panties. She quickly tied the robe and slowly walked to the end of the sofa.

He was smiling. She wasn't sure if it was just his patented signature or in his mind, he was like the big bad wolf, licking his chops because of what he saw beneath the robe. He beckoned to her and patted the back of the sofa, indicating for her to sit.

Toni sat holding her robe closed at the base of her neck. "What do you want to share with me?" she asked.

He rubbed the palms of his hands together. "I want to share the world with you."

Toni smiled. "The world? I didn't even realize that you owned it."

"Not entirely," he replied, "but I believe you deserve everything that your heart yearns for."

Quickly Toni replied, "My heart never actually spoke to anyone about my yearnings. I've had only one yearning, and as a child I dreamed of it often. Guess what? That dream came true. I'm living it now. I don't need anything else."

"But are you happy?" he asked sincerely.

Toni shrugged, "Of course. Why wouldn't I be?"

He reached over and took her hand, "Oh, such softness."

She drew her hand back.

"Toni, when was the last time you were held in someone's arms, caressed, and told that you meant the world to them? When were you told that the essence of your beauty sparked the lifeline, making a man want to live forever? When was the last time you were kissed with such passion that you felt your heart would leap right out of your chest and beg for the moment to never pass?"

Toni had almost become mesmerized by his words. She looked at him, but wasn't looking at him. He seemed different. Not a threat, but someone reaching out to heal. "Toni, Toni, my dear. Let me take you where you've never gone before."

Toni got up and started to pace the floor. "What exactly is it that you want from me?"

He stood and moved towards her. His fingers ran through her hair as he gently caressed her. "You are such a wonder of beauty." Then he pulled her face to his and kissed her lightly on the lips, waiting to see if she would respond.

Toni's eyes were closed. She moved forward with anticipation, pressing her lips to his. She pressed harder at his mouth as her arms went up about his shoulders. His arms went around her waist. He felt her heavy breathing, her heart pounding. He took her arms away from around his neck, stepped back, and admired her. She stood there shaking like a leaf on a limb. Unbeknown to her, her robe had opened, revealing her perfectly sculpted body. He looked at her heaving breasts. Then Jean's eyes went downward to her stomach and south. The flatness of her abdomen excited him and filled his mind with lustful anticipation.

Toni opened her eyes and looked at him. His eyes were filled with desire, his smile and lips intriguing. Gently, he took her by the hand and led her to the sofa, seating her while he reached for the bottle of champagne.

"Let us toast this night, my dear. A night of new beginnings. A night of pleasure."

Toni sat wide-eyed. She didn't know what to expect, but at that moment, she really didn't care.

chapter twenty-three

The Seduction

THEY BOTH CHATTED BACK AND forth, drinking the champagne, musing over one another. Toni was sitting in his lap, her arm around his neck. She would sip champagne, then press her lips to his, opening their mouths to allow the liquid to enter into his. She giggled, he laughed. She fell gracefully to the floor, lying on her back, still giggling. She was like a young teenage girl, exploring all the possibilities. He sat looking down at her. Then she stretched out her arms to him. "Come," she whispered. Jean stood, took off his jacket, unbuttoned his shirt, and slung them on the sofa. He lay down next to her and stroked the side of her face.

"I don't understand what it is that makes me want you to be a part of me. I just know, right now, I need you."

Toni giggled, rising slightly to give him a kiss. "You just want to get in my pants, that's all."

He didn't look surprised but said, "That would be nice, but I really want to get into *you*."

The champagne had Toni's head swirling. "I bet you do!" He kissed her on the lips. She squirmed, "This is uncomfortable."

He whispered, "For me too." He stood up and extended his hand to pull her up. She almost fell. In a swoop, he had picked her up safely into his arms. Her arms were wrapped around his neck.

"Where are you taking me?" she asked.

"Where do you want to go?" he replied.

"Take me to the mountain!"

He looked at her strangely, "To the mountain?"

She turned toward the bedroom. He smiled, "Oh, *that* mountain." They entered the bedroom, and he sat on the bed while she pretended to waltz to music he was sure that only she heard. Toni stopped in front of him and let her robe drop to the floor. Then she unbuttoned her bra and let it fall on top of the robe. Next, she worked her way out of her panties and they, too, lay with the other garments.

Jean could only stare while the muscles in his neck twitched along with other muscles elsewhere in his body. Hastily, he stood up and unbuckled his trousers. In fact, he almost tripped over one pants leg in an effort to free himself. There he stood in his expensive silk boxers. She pushed him back onto the bed and straddled him. He looked up at her and said, "Let me take my shorts off."

Toni pressed her finger to his lips. "Not yet, not just yet." With that, she got up and walked to the bedroom closet, where she retrieved a sheer white gown and put it on. Then she walked over to the vanity and sat down, casually brushing her hair while watching him in the mirror. He appeared perplexed. She turned toward him. "I don't use any type of birth control method. Do you have a condom?"

Jean walked over to her. "Of course, my darling. It's essential that one must." He kissed her on the forehead.

Toni got up and went to the bathroom. "I'm going to take a shower. I shouldn't be long."

When she disappeared into the bathroom, Jean took off his shorts and climbed into the king-sized bed, stretched out his arms, cracked his knuckles, and lay back against the oversized pillow, waiting. At that moment, the phone rang. He looked at it. It continued to ring. He looked toward the bathroom. The water was running, so he assumed Toni was still showering. Without a second thought, he picked up the receiver. "Hello?"

The voice on the other end asked, "Who is this?"

He asked, "Whom do you wish to speak to?"

"This is Liz. Where's Toni?"

"She's in the shower."

"What the hell is she doing in the shower?"

"Taking a shower, I suppose."

Liz almost yelled. "What the hell is going on over there?"

Jean smiled to himself. "We're having a party."

"Bullshit," Liz screamed. "Tell Toni I'm coming over!"

Jean recommended otherwise. "It's not appropriate that you do."

Liz slammed down the receiver.

Jean spoke to himself, "My, she's real chummy."

chapter twenty-four:
Confrontation

TONI CAME OUT OF THE bathroom wrapped in a towel. Her scent was strong and sweet. Her caramel body glistened with beads of still-dripping water. "Did I hear the phone ring?" she asked, looking at Jean.

He was looking at her like a dog hungry for a bone, of course with meat on it. "Wrong number."

Toni walked to the dresser, brushed her hair briefly, sprayed on some perfumed mist, seductively walked to the bed, let the towel drop, and climbed in. She cuddled closely to Jean. He put his arm across her breasts as she looked into his eyes with innocence, yet filled with passion that was long overdue. He slid his hand over her body, letting it move slowly down her leg. He felt her squirm. She tensed for a moment, then relaxed. He threw the covers back, exposing themselves to one another.

She nibbled at his earlobe, and he kissed the nipple of her breast gently.

She whispered, "Where's the condom?"

He continued kissing her breast. "I have it on."

"Are you sure?" she asked.

"Would I lie to you?" he asked blatantly.

She smiled, "Would you?"

He mounted her and passionately nibbled on her neck while they gave themselves over to pure lust. Then, there was a loud and continuous knock at the door. Toni bolted upright and said, "Someone's at the door."

Jean pulled her back down. "Who cares who it is."

The knocking continued. Toni got up and slipped on her robe. "It might be important. I won't be but a minute." Looking through the peephole, she saw Liz, looking like an angry, wounded lioness. "Oh, shit!" Toni said, again surprising herself.

Liz started hitting the door this time, yelling. "Toni, Toni, open this door! Do you hear me? Open this door this minute!"

People on the floor started peeking out from behind their doors. One rudely awakened man asked, "What the hell is going on? People are trying to sleep around here. Take that crap to a bar or some back alley."

Liz turned, not sure who was talking, and extended out her middle finger. "Go suck a tit," she angrily yelled. Then she continued her attack on Toni's door. Someone called security.

Shortly, two security personnel arrived. They surveyed the scene, attempting to get a full visual of what was taking place. "What's going on here?" one demanded.

Liz turned to see a muscular black man giving her a menacing look. The other security officer, who was white, said to Liz, "Ma'am, you're causing a commotion. You need to calm down and go to your room."

Liz looked at him sternly. "Do you know who the hell I am?"

Both security officers looked at each other, then at Liz, and said in unison, "We don't give a damn. Shut it down or we call NYPD."

At that moment, Toni opened the door. "It's alright, officers. I can handle this. Sorry for the disturbance."

She pulled Liz into the suite and quickly closed the door. Liz stood in the center of the floor, visibly upset. Toni stood with her arms folded, looking at Liz in disbelief. "What in the world is wrong with you?"

Liz gritted her teeth while shaking her finger at Toni. "How could you? Toni, have you lost your mind?"

Toni opened her hands with palms up, questioning, "What, Liz? What's going on?"

Liz bit down on her lower lip. "I thought you had a splitting headache. I thought you weren't feeling so well. I thought you were just going to get some rest. This is totally bullshit! Where is he, Toni?"

Toni sighed, "Liz, please. Calm down. This is not necessary."

"The hell you say. Look at you. You're damn near naked."

Liz looked around and saw the champagne bottle on the floor. She walked to the sofa and picked up Jean's jacket and shirt. "Who does *this* belong to? The maintenance man? What's he been doing—fixing your plumbing?"

Just then, Jean walked out of the bedroom in all his glory. "What's all the fuss about?" he asked while trying to focus his eyes.

Shocked, Liz looked at him standing there in the nude. Her hand flew to her mouth. She looked at Toni, who had lowered her head. "I *don't* believe this!"

Jean smiled. "You must be Liz." He extended his hand towards her. Liz drew back. She walked over to Toni, looked her in the eyes and said, "Everything you worked hard for, the humiliation you encountered, the trials and tribulations we both endured—I embraced you when the world only admired you.

They paid to look at your beauty. I gave my heart and soul to you because I loved you as my own. Toni, you have put a scar upon my heart that I think will never be removed." She spun around and walked promptly to the door.

Toni called out to her. "Liz, I'm only human. I need more in my life than just to be looked at. I want to feel the warmth of someone's arms around me, to look at me and really see *me*—not as some *thing* from another world that everyone is amazed about. I'm a woman with feelings, like any other human be-ing. Can't you possibly understand that?"

Liz turned to see tears streaming down Toni's face. She harshly snapped, "Clean up your mess. We'll talk tomorrow." Then she looked at Jean with contempt. "I suggest you gather your belongings and find another cave to hibernate in." That said, she stormed out.

chapter twenty-five—
Lost in Thought

Jean walked over to Toni and attempted to console her. "My dear, Toni, come to bed. I will dry your tears."

Toni looked at the clock on the wall. It was 2:20 a.m. "I think you should go. Right now, I need to be alone."

He looked at her pitifully. "Maybe that's been the problem. You've been alone for too long." He attempted to put his arms around her, but she pushed him away.

"Please, Jean, I really need to be by myself."

Resigned, he picked up his jacket and shirt and walked into the bedroom. Minutes later he reappeared, fully dressed. He paused to look at her, then walked to the door. He turned to see her sitting on the sofa with her knees drawn to her chin.

"Toni," he called, but she didn't respond, so he left, gently closing the door behind him.

Toni was still sitting on the sofa when a ray of light peeked through the partially separated drapes. "How long have I been sitting here?" she asked herself, dazed. The clock on the wall read 6 a.m.

Deciding on a cup of tea, she got up and went into the kitchen and began to boil a kettle of water. In her mind, she was struggling, trying to fit the pieces to a puzzle. Where had she gone wrong? After steeping the cup of tea, she went into the bedroom and stared at the bed. She wondered, "How could I?" while her other mind assured her, "It's okay! No harm, no foul." She shook her head. "No! I was taught better." She pulled the covers back on the bed. Nothing! She looked beneath the bed. Nothing! She went to the wastebasket. Nothing!

Her heart began to pound. She put the cup of tea on the dresser. *It has to be here somewhere,* she thought. Frantically, she looked all over the room. Nothing! Her worst nightmare was becoming a reality. She whispered, "There *has* to be an empty package to show that he used a condom, but nothing!"

She tried to convince herself that she was just being paranoid. "Maybe he put the packet in his pocket after he got dressed," she tried to reason.

She still felt an uneasiness in the pit of her stomach. She needed to talk to Liz, to make things right. She wanted to explain to her that it was just a moment of passion and she just got caught up. She went to the phone, reached for the receiver, then promptly drew her hand away. She was reluctant. Actually, she was afraid. *How can I face her?* she thought. "I know, I'll take a hot shower first, then I'll call."

Fifteen minutes later, Toni stepped out of the shower and patted herself dry. She walked to the mirror and looked at herself. She felt she looked different. She didn't see the beauty that so many admired. What she saw was what she was feeling—guilt. Just then, her stomach growled, indicating that she should eat something. After looking at the phone directory for room service, she dialed.

"Room service, may I help you?" the voice greeted her.

"Yes. This is Ms. Morrison in suite seven thirty-two."

"Yes, Ms. Morrison, how can we help you this morning?"

"May I order two pieces of rye toast, a half grapefruit, and a cup of cottage cheese?"

"Will that be all?"

"Yes, thank you."

The voice cheerfully replied, "It will be there shortly. Have a nice day."

Toni hung up the receiver, then turned on the TV as she sat on the edge of the bed. Surfing the channels, she glanced at several church programs. Interestingly, she tuned in on one program and started to listen intently to what the speaker was saying. "God loves you, even when you may think that no one else does. He will forgive you when there are those who will not. There's nothing so drastic that can occur in your life that He will not forgive you. Open up your heart and receive Him today. He's knocking at the door of your heart. He knows your pain, your discomfort, and He's calling you right now."

Toni felt awkward. Something stirred inside of her. Suddenly, there was a knock at the door. "Yes?" she replied.

"Room service, Ma'am."

Toni went to the door and opened it. A young man stood there with a cart and a tray containing the items she had ordered. Toni stepped back and allowed the young man to bring the tray into the room. "Just sign here, Ma'am," he said, giving her a slip of paper.

Toni signed and smiled, "Thank you."

He saluted her and strolled away, whistling a tune, closing the door behind him.

After eating, Toni began to feel better. She went to the phone, briefly hesitated, then quickly dialed Liz's extension. The phone rang and rang. Toni started to hang up when she heard, "Hello?"

chapter twenty-six—
Making Up

Toni hesitated while Liz again said, "Hello?" Finally, she worked up enough nerve to speak. "Liz?" This was followed by silence. Toni cleared her throat and began again. "Liz, I'm sorry. Can we talk? Please!"

The silence became deafening. "I know you're upset with me, but please give me a chance to explain. Liz, are you there?"

Liz spoke. "I'm here."

Toni closed her eyes and sighed a breath of relief. "Can you come over?"

Liz spoke evenly, "No, I won't come over to your suite." She paused. "But you can come over to mine."

Toni smiled, "That'll be great. I'll be there in ten minutes."

Liz said, "You better make it fifteen. I'm still getting my groove on."

Toni said, "What?"

Liz chuckled, "I'm just kidding; see you in ten."

Ten minutes later, Toni stood at Liz's suite door. She took a deep breath before knocking. After the second knock, Liz opened the door. Toni just stood there, smiling nervously. Liz looked at her without expression, then said curtly, "Come in."

Toni entered while she kept her eyes on Liz, trying to read her body language. "Have a seat," Liz said, pointing to the sofa. Toni sat down nervously. Liz asked, "You want some coffee or tea?"

Toni shook her head. "I had breakfast already."

Liz sat across from her holding what appeared to be a cup of coffee. She moved back in the sofa chair, crossed her leg, looked at Toni, and said, "Well?"

Toni felt awkward. "Liz, I'm sorry. I really am. If you would just forgive me."

Liz leaned forward. "Who was that jerk? Where did he come from? Why was he in your bedroom naked? Don't tell me. Let me guess."

Toni bit down on her lower lip. "I met him the other night at the fashion session. He came backstage to my dressing room. Earlier, I had seen him out front in the audience. He wanted to spend a few moments with me, but I told him I was tired. He was insistent, but I told him no. When I left the theatre and was walking, a limo pulled up. It was him. He convinced me to have a late-night meal and chat.

Shortly afterwards, he walked me to my suite. I didn't invite him in though."

Liz raised a brow, "And?"

Toni continued. "He called me, and we talked for a few minutes."

Liz sat her coffee on the end table. "Malcom told me about the limo and some guy persuading you to get in with him."

Toni looked surprised. "He told you that?"

Liz rubbed her forehead. "Malcom takes his job very seriously."

"So, I really shouldn't be surprised," Toni said disdainfully.

Liz rubbed her hands together, "Toni, I'm just trying to protect you. That's one of my primary responsibilities. I was hired as your confidant, primarily because of my background in fashion and modeling. However, I assumed you wanted more than that, so I became what one would view as a den mother of sorts. Sweetheart, you've been blessed to come as far as you have. It's a mean world out there. Predators are lurking everywhere. I realize you want something else besides your career, but it's difficult to try and balance both. I'm not stupid. You're a woman. You've got that need that most women have. You want to be loved, in a mental sense as well as a physical one. Hell, even I do at times. You just need to be sure you come across the right one.

"Men! Oh my God! What can I say? They aren't all dogs, but they certainly have the same bark. Do you understand what I'm trying to tell you?"

Toni nodded, "I think I do."

Liz sighed. "Toni, the time *will* come and then you will know it's the right time. You'll get married, have a bunch of kids, and live the life of a dotting mother. You're still young. You still have your career. Take your time, enjoy the rewards of your success. I ain't no saint, but I've learned enough to know good things will come to those who wait. I was once young and foolish. Rushed into marriage because I let my eyes deceive me and my emotions get in the way. Thank God, I didn't come up pregnant."

Why did she say that? Toni thought.

"Anyway, Liz still loves you. Oh, by the way, I've booked our flight out for tomorrow. It's on to Copenhagen, then to Tokyo, then back to the States. We'll have two weeks in between. How about I call Mom and Dad and tell them to meet us in Hawaii? We all can stand to relax a bit."

Toni smiled. "That sounds wonderful! Liz, you're the greatest."

Liz smiled, "I'm good for something."

chapter twenty-seven

Hawaii, Here We Come

Toni and Liz flew around the globe. Toni did shows and the people loved her everywhere, admiring her stunning beauty on and off the catwalk. Of course, Liz played it up, enticing crowd after crowd to see the most extravagant model in the world.

Now in the air once again, Toni rested her head against the back of her seat. The flight attendant asked, "Would you like to have a pillow?"

Toni turned to her, "I'm fine, thank you."

The flight attendant said, "I heard the fashion show was a success in Tokyo."

Liz butted in, "It was unbelievable. The Japanese people loved her. They couldn't get enough. By the way, you're strikingly beautiful yourself. You ever thought about modeling?"

The attendant smiled, "I did a little modeling a few years back. I'm afraid it didn't pan out very well."

"Ah, what a shame," Liz said sincerely. "Can you do me a favor?"

The attendant smiled. "Sure."

Liz looked over at Toni to see that she still had her eyes closed. She whispered to the attendant, "Please bring me a gin with a twist of lime."

The attendant nodded and walked off. Liz reached in the magazine rack and pulled out a glamour magazine. Flipping through several pages, she came upon Toni's picture and an article about the fashion world.

The plane suddenly bounced when it hit an air pocket that startled Liz. She looked around to see if any of the other passengers were anxious. By then, the flight attendant had brought her gin. "Here you are, Ma'am."

"Thank you," Liz said. Unexpectedly, the plane vibrated and buckled for a moment. Liz tensed up. She motioned to the attendant. "Are we going through some bad weather?"

The attendant smiled and assured her it was just a little turbulence. "We'll be fine."

Liz turned to see Toni smiling. "It's my nerves," Liz commented.

"Yeah, I know," Toni replied.

"I can't wait to see Mom and Dad. That was a great idea for you to have them meet us in Hawaii. They needed to get away for a while. When is the next fashion show?"

Liz looked in her planning guide. "We go to Sydney in three weeks. Then it's on to Miami."

The plane buckled once again. "With all the flying we've done, this is beginning to work my nerves," Liz complained.

Toni patted her on the knee. "Courage, my friend, courage."

"I probably need another drink," Liz muttered, hoping that Toni would agree.

"Liz, you don't need another drink. You need to relax. Take a deep breath, then exhale."

Liz looked at Toni as though she had lost her mind. "I'll exhale after we land."

The flight attendant asked, "Is everything OK?"

Liz asked, "When will we be arriving in Hawaii?"

The attendant looked at her watch. "In less than an hour."

Toni asked Liz, "Mom and Dad are staying at the Hawaiian Hilton, right?"

Liz nodded. The plane buckled.

After the planed leveled again, Liz unfastened her seat belt and got up hurriedly. "Where you going?" Toni asked.

Without looking back, Liz said, "I gotta pee!" Toni looked out the window of the plane and watched the clouds easily pass by. She was full of anticipation in wanting to see her parents.

Liz returned from the restroom and seated herself, "Damn restrooms! How can a plane be so big and have a toilet just big enough for a midget to sit on?"

"Are we booked at the Hilton too?" Toni asked.

"No," Liz said, trying to keep from smiling. "We got a hut on Maui Beach." She pinched Toni. "Of course, we are."

Toni thought to herself, *This woman is too much at times. But I just love her to death anyway.*

"Ladies and gentlemen, please take your seats. We'll be landing shortly. We would like to take this opportunity and thank you for flying with us. The weather on the islands range from seventy to about eighty degrees. We hope you enjoy your stay in the Hawaiian Islands," a voice said over the intercom.

Thump! The landing gear of the plane came down with a thud.

"I hope one of the damn wheels didn't come off," Liz snapped.

Toni shook her head as she thought, *This woman doesn't ever stop.*

The tires screeched as the plane touched down on the runway. Loud noise filled the cabin as the jet engines whistled and the plane began to slow down.

"Please remain seated until the plane has come to a full stop," the voice on the intercom continued.

Liz sighed, "Finally! My butt is aching."

The plane stopped at the disembarking platform. As ever, passengers started bustling about, retrieving bags from the overhead compartments. Liz got up and motioned for Toni. "Let's go!"

"Liz, we're here. Take your time."

"Yes, we're here, so let's get the hell off," Liz replied, struggling with the bags in the overhead compartment.

"Need some help?"

She turned to see a tall, handsome black man standing behind her, towering over her. Liz forgot about the bags for a moment, staring into his striking face and admiring his beautiful, even white teeth. His dimpled cheeks and his hazel eyes captivated her.

Oh, my goodness, she thought. *I hope he's staying at our hotel.*

"I can help you with those if you like," he offered.

Liz whispered to herself, "You can help me with more than just those bags."

"You're such a gentleman, thank you," she said, then looked at Toni with a mischievous grin. Before long, they entered the terminal. Liz paused to thank the tall gentleman.

"It was my pleasure," he smiled, then turned to walk away.

Liz called out, "My name is Elizabeth."

He smiled and extended his hand. "I'm Jermaine, Jermaine Taylor."

Liz rested her diminutive hand in his oversized one. "Oh, yes. You're that professional basketball player."

He smiled. "I got to go. I have someone waiting on me."

Liz swallowed, thinking, *I hope it's only a cab.*

He couldn't disappear among the crowds of people because of his height. Liz just stood there, watching his head until it was no longer visible. When she turned to Toni, she was no longer there. "What the—" she started to say, then she observed Toni in the arms of her parents.

chapter twenty-eight
Mai Tais and Dancing

LIZ LAZILY CARRIED THE BAGS toward Toni and her parents just as Lester, Toni's father, walked up to her and threw his arms around her. "How are you, my dear? You look as fine as ever."

Liz kissed him on the cheek, then went and hugged Gina. "Mama Morrison, you look fantastic. How have you been?"

Gina smiled. "Now that both of my girls are here, this is going to be a great vacation. I'm so happy to see you. And, you, too, my little angel," she said, looking at Toni.

Liz playfully rolled her eyes at Toni. Toni smiled back and stuck her tongue out at Liz. "Let me get these bags," Lester said. "There's a shuttle out front that will take us to the hotel."

After a short ride, they arrived at the hotel. "Why don't you girls rest up and get settled, then we all can go have some dinner," Gina suggested.

"Sounds good to me," Liz returned. "My behind is aching from sitting so long on that plane. I need to soak in some Hawaiian Epsom salts and pineapple juice." They all laughed.

After several hours of resting, they all joined up in the hotel lobby and took a cab to the Maui-Mau Restaurant. Once arriving, they entered and were seated immediately. It was packed. Most of the tables were full. The four of them looked around at the island decor. Lit Tiki torches burned, giving a romantic overtone to the dining rooms. Gina joyfully rubbed Lester on his arm. Dancers on the stage twirled fiery batons. Men wearing colorful Aloha shirts and women wearing vibrant sarong skirts danced barefoot with precision and in unison.

They were brought menus by two beautiful island girls dressed in hula skirts who placed the traditional flowers around everyone's neck and greeted them with "Aloha."

One of the girls walked away with her hips swinging gracefully. Lester smiled. Toni nudged her mother. "Mom, you better keep an eye on Dad. You don't want him getting loose in here." They all smiled, ordered drinks, and casually chatted while watching the stage performances. Liz was enjoying her Mai Tai cocktail so much, she was actually moving to the beat of the drums while sitting in her chair.

"Somebody's feeling pretty good," Gina said as they looked at Liz.

"This drink is wonderful. You should try it," she said, looking at them.

Toni asked, "Liz, isn't that your friend? The guy you met on the plane?"

Liz looked around and said, "Where?"

Toni said, "Look to your left." Liz turned, and there he was.

Her eyes bulged with excitement as she took another sip of her drink. "Y'all have to excuse me. I'm going over to say hi to a dear friend."

Toni sighed, "Oh-oh."

Lester and Gina looked at each other in surprise. Liz walked over to the table where the athlete sat. "Hi, there!" she said, attempting to be as charming as possible.

He studied her for a moment. "Oh! The lady from the plane. I see you made it alright. You having din-ner?" he asked.

Liz was at a loss for words for a second. "Yes, I'm with some friends" and nodded towards their table.

"That's nice" he said. "By the way, this is Michelle, my fiancée. Michelle, this is ..." he paused. "What was your name again?"

"Elizabeth, but everyone calls me Liz."

"Oh, that's right." He shrugged. "Well, Liz, I'm sure you don't want to keep your friends waiting. It was nice seeing you again though."

Liz looked at the beautiful girl. "It was nice meeting you."

"Likewise," the young lady responded.

Liz turned to go back to the table when the athlete called out, "Hey, Liz, enjoy your dinner and the show."

As Liz approached the table, her friends could see the sad look on her face. She attempted to look pleasant, however, but Toni was reading her as ever before. No one said anything for a moment. Then the beating of loud drums got everybody's attention. The announcer said, "We're going to have some of our visiting guests from the mainland and around the world come up on stage and dance with the lovely hula girls. Who would like to come on up?"

Everyone smiled or giggled, hoping someone else in their group would go up and make a clown of themselves. But no one moved. The announcer said, "How about this lovely couple?" pointing at Lester and Gina.

"Uh-uh," Lester said.

"Go on, Dad" Toni urged.

Two dancers from the stage, a girl and guy, danced over to their table. The girl took Lester by the hand, the guy took Gina by the hand and led them to the stage. Everyone applauded. Toni laughed heartily while watching her parents struggle in their effort to do the hula. After a few moments, Lester waved his hand goodbye as he exited the stage. He came back to the table almost exhausted. "I should have brought my Geritol," he said smiling.

"How about some applause for the gentleman," the announcer said warmly. The people applauded, and Toni kissed him on the cheek. "You did good, Dad."

They looked at Gina who continued to dance. "Mom is really doing great," Toni said admiringly.

"That she is," Lester marveled. When the music finished, Gina left the stage to an enthusiastic round of applause. She sighed as she came back to the table. "My goodness! I'm going to have to sit in a hot tub for a week."

Lester kissed her on the cheek. "You did great, honey."

They all looked at Liz who appeared somber. "Liz, you want to try and give it a shot?" Lester asked.

She wiped at the corner of her eyes. "Excuse me," she said as she rose from the table and walked out of the restaurant. Toni attempted to go after her, but Lester said, "Stay here with your mom. I'll go get her."

chapter twenty-nine

A Private Talk

LESTER WALKED A SHORT DISTANCE before he observed Liz standing under .a palm tree, looking out toward the beach. He quietly walked up to her. "Liz, are you alright?" he asked.

She just stood there motionless. He put his hand on her shoulder. "Liz, what is it?"

She turned to him. "I just don't understand."

"What is it that you don't understand?"

"I'm not that old. I don't think that I'm that unattractive. Why isn't it that I can't find someone to give my life to? Toni has been and will continue to be a huge part of my life, but I need someone that I can truly call my own. Lester, you and Gina have something that is rarely found in people today. You both genuinely care for each other. The love you both have for one another surpasses anything I've come to know. I've seen you both withstand the turbulence of keeping your love strong for each other in spite of the degradation, the racism, the prejudice, and the insults. Through it all, you both have managed to stay afloat. It has to be more than just courage. That's real love. I admire you both. That's all I want, just to be loved."

Lester pulled her head to his shoulder. "I know. But you mustn't ever give up. It's a challenge that few will ever be able to sustain. We live in a crazy world, full of hatred, bitterness, and pure evil. But I've always believed that if people, were just to look a little deeper to allow their hearts to move instead of their emotions, they would find peace, love, and tolerance that they could share with other individuals. We're not perfect. But at least if we all just make a continuing effort, I believe things would be much better. Listen to your heart, Liz. Don't act upon your emotions. Ask God to give you the courage and the guidance to see you through. I do every day. I have to. If Gina leaves me, I don't know what I'll do."

Liz looked at him curiously. "Gina would never leave you. Why would you even think that? You two have been together for years. There is no reason for her to leave you. You're a good man, Lester, and Gina knows it. She loves you too much."

Concerned and surprised, Liz saw tears in his eyes. "Lester, you're not crying?"

He squeezed her hand. "Promise me, Liz, promise me you will never tell Toni."

Liz looked mystified. "Promise what? Not tell Toni what?"

"Liz, Gina has breast cancer!"

Liz almost fell backwards. Lester held on to her to keep her from falling. She stood there, wide-eyed in disbelief.

"Oh, Lester, no! What are the doctors saying? What medical treatment are they providing? How far along is it?"

Lester shook his head in almost disbelief himself. "She's been going for treatment, but it seems as if she's getting weaker. She's strong in her own right, but I can see it's taking its toll on her. Of course, no one else would be able to see it as I do. Gina is a fighter, and I know she will fight right up to the end, win or lose."

"And Toni doesn't know?" Liz asked incredulously.

Lester wiped at his brow, "Gina doesn't want her to know, at least not now. She believes it will interfere with Toni's career. We both waited a long time to see her dream finally come true. There's something else I want you to promise me, Liz. If anything happens to either of us, will you look after Toni as much as possible?"

Liz nodded tearfully. "I promise, I promise."

Lester wiped the tears from her eyes with his handkerchief. "We can't go back and let them see the tears, now, can we?"

Liz smiled, "No."

Walking to the entrance of the restaurant, they noticed Toni and Gina standing outside. Toni shouted, "There they are. We thought you two got lost. We were getting ready to send out the pineapple patrol," she giggled.

"Is everything OK?" Gina asked.

Lester smiled, "Everything's just fine."

chapter thirty

Off to Sydney

THE TWO WEEKS WENT BY quickly, too quickly, in fact, and then it was time to go. They were the most enjoyable two weeks Toni had spent with her parents since she was a child and the three of them took a trip to the Bahamas. They all rode in silence to the airport. Toni coughed.

"Are you alright, sweetheart?" her mother asked.

"I'm fine, Mom. My throat is just a little scratchy."

"I hope you're not coming down with anything," Gina added.

"She'll be alright," Liz said convincingly.

Once in the terminal, they chatted awhile longer until they heard a voice on the intercom announce, "Passengers boarding for Sydney, please report to Gate B."

Toni hugged her mom and kissed her. She turned to her dad, saying, "I love you, Dad. Take good care of Mom for me." She kissed him and hugged him tightly.

Liz kissed Gina on the cheek and hugged her. She stared at Lester for a moment, remembering what he had told her. "Thank you for giving me the courage." She kissed him on the cheek as Toni stood there, admiring her parents.

Gina's eyes became teary. "We love you, baby. Be sure to let us hear from you."

"I will," Toni assured them. She ran to them and hugged them both once more.

"Go, or you'll miss your flight," Lester said, trying desperately not to show emotion.

Liz and Toni boarded the plane. As the plane backed away from the ramp, Lester put his arms around his wife. They stood looking out the big glass window, seeing the plane go down the runway for takeoff. Gina whispered, "There goes our baby."

***

TWICE DURING THE flight, Toni went to the restroom. "What's wrong with you?" Liz asked.

"I had to go to the restroom," Toni replied.

Liz looked at her strangely. "You threw up several times while we were in Hawaii. The food didn't agree with you?"

"I guess not," Toni replied somewhat sheepishly.

Liz stretched her arms over her head. "Sometimes I feel like I'm getting too old for this." She turned to Toni for a response, but she had her eyes closed. Liz motioned for the flight attendant. "Excuse me. Can I get some service?"

The attendant smiled, "Of course. What would you like to have?"

Liz ran her tongue across her lips. "How about a gin and tonic?"

"Would there be anything else you'd like?" the attendant asked.

"That will be fine for now," Liz answered. After receiving her drink, Liz stretched out her legs and tilted her seat back. "Might as well get as comfortable as possible," she mused.

After an hour into the flight, Liz became irate because the passenger behind her was snoring very loudly. She turned, wanting to say something to the man, but then she thought better. *No need to start a commotion*, she thought. She reasoned with herself, "I know, another drink will help resolve this issue." With that thought in mind, she pushed the call button for service.

The attendant arrived. "Yes, Madam?"

Liz rubbed her hands together. "Please bring me a gin and tonic, please."

"Of course," the attendant said. "I won't be but a moment."

Twenty minutes later, the attendant still hadn't returned with Liz's drink. She finally became impatient. Once again, she pushed the button for service. She waited, but there was no response. She pushed the button a second time and finally an attendant arrived. This was a different person than previously. "May I help you?" she asked.

Liz was attempting to control her breathing. "I asked for a gin and tonic more than twenty minutes ago. Why haven't I received it?"

The attendant said, "I'm awfully sorry. The other attendant may have forgotten or was busy with other passengers."

Liz said to herself, "What the hell do you think that I am? *I'm* a passenger."

The attendant continued, "I'll go get it for you right now."

In less than two minutes she was back with the drink. "Here you are, Madam. I'm sorry for the inconvenience."

Liz nodded, "Thank you."

The attendant moved on down the aisle, smiling at passengers. "Now *that's* what I'm talking about," Liz said to no one in particular. She sipped the drink and let it ooze down her throat slowly. Afterwards, she turned to see an elderly gentleman looking at her, smiling. "What?" Liz said somewhat harshly.

He quickly turned away to look at his magazine that was lying in his lap. Liz sipped her drink and thought, *Old geezer is probably trying to make some play.* In a few moments, she, too, would let her eyes fall to slumber like her companion.

Toni had awakened. She complained that she was not feeling well. She nudged Liz, who awoke, startled, "What? Did a wing come off the plane?" she looked at Toni and saw the concerned look on her face. "What is it, honey?" she asked.

Toni lay her head back and said, "I'm not feeling well."

Liz turned to put her hand on Toni's forehead. "You don't feel warm. What's wrong?" Liz asked.

"My stomach feels kind of queasy."

"You want a seltzer? It may help settle your stomach."

"I guess, if it might help."

After the attendant was called, Toni drank the seltzer and settled back to rest.

After disembarking and checking into their hotel, the two of them toured the city, taking in the sights. "Oh, my!" Toni said delightedly. "Sydney is beautiful. I wouldn't mind living here." Men observed them wherever they went, perfecting smiles that they hoped would be luring and inviting. Liz just snarled at most of them. Toni was fascinated with the people's Australian accent. "Is it English that they derived their language from? I mean, the Queen's English?"

"Hell, I don't know," Liz answered. "I know they ain't German."

They stopped at a boutique shop, went in, and browsed around. A salesclerk watched them as they moved about. Liz spotted the salesgirl looking at them "You see that?" she asked Toni.

"See what, Liz?" Toni asked.

"That girl is watching us."

Toni turned to see the girl smiling. "Oh, Liz, she probably knows we're American tourists."

"I'm telling you, she's looking at us as if we're going to steal something."

"Liz, why must you always have to be in the negative zone about things?"

The girl walked over to them. In the strongest accent they had yet to hear, she asked, "Can I help you with something?"

Toni smiled at her, "We're just looking. It's our first time to Australia so we're just out and about."

The girl continued looking at Toni. Liz turned to the girl. "You haven't anything better to do?"

"Liz!" Toni almost rebuked her. "Where's your manners?"

Liz frowned, "I left them in America."

"Don't mind her," Toni told the clerk. "She's been ill since she came into the world."

"Funny, very funny," Liz said disdainfully.

The girl smiled, "I recognize you!"

Liz turned to her, "Who me?"

"No," the girl replied. "Her!" pointing at Toni. "I've seen you in the magazines. You're an actress, right?"

Liz laughed out loud.

chapter thirty-one ▬
The Flight Home

THE FASHION SHOW WAS A success, as usual. Toni was intrigued by the other models. "Oh! They were so beautiful," she gushed.

"Not as beautiful as you were," Liz countered. "By the way, I couldn't help but notice, but it seems you're gaining a little weight in your hips. You haven't been eating any kangaroo meat since we've been here, have you?" she chuckled.

When Toni didn't respond, she continued, "Well, my dear, I've had about all of Australia that I can stand. I'm ready to get back to the good ol' U.S. of A. How about you? Ready for that long flight?"

Toni sighed deeply, "I guess so."

On the flight home, Toni asked, "When are we suppose to do Miami?"

Liz shrugged. "We'll have a week before the setup, I guess. I suppose you're going to your mom and dad's house when we get back?"

"Why do you ask me that?" Toni inquired.

"Well, I was wondering because you just saw them in Hawaii and I thought maybe you would want to go to Vegas with me."

"Vegas? Are you kidding? I wouldn't be caught dead down there," Toni replied, matter-of-factly.

Liz looked at her as if she had just landed from another planet. "*Everybody* goes to Vegas. What dimension are you living in? I can hear Elvis singing "Viva Las Vegas.""

Toni looked at her with uncertainty. "You sure can hear extremely well then, 'cause I can't hear anything."

"You're funny, really funny, Toni. You ever thought about being a fashion clown?"

"Only if you would manage me," she laughed.

The plane buckled and swayed a bit. *Oh, not again,* Liz thought. Toni gagged a little. "Are you OK?" Liz asked.

"I feel nauseous," Toni answered.

"These damn planes," Liz grumbled. She pushed the call button for an attendant.

The attendant arrived promptly and asked, "Yes? What can I do for you?"

Liz inquired, "Can you bring something for her?" nodding at Toni. "She has an upset stomach. Oh, by the way, bring me a gin and tonic. I have a serious headache." She turned to Toni and winked.

The attendant said, "I'll be back in a moment."

Toni rose from her seat.

"Where're you going?" Liz asked.

"I have to use the restroom," Toni replied while hurrying past Liz.

Liz thought, *Damn, that girl pisses more than a Jamaican bull that's excited.* She laughed to herself. "Where the hell did I come up with that one?"

Toni came back and seated herself.

"How do you feel?" Liz asked.

"Much better," Toni replied, trying not to acknowledge her.

Liz chuckled, "There ain't nothing like taking a good ol' piss."

Toni shook her head. "You're unbelievable."

"What?" Liz said laughing to herself.

"Here's your drinks," the flight attendant said. She handed Toni hers. "I hope this will make you feel better."

"Thank you," Toni responded.

"Here's yours, Ma'am," she stated, handing Liz the plastic glass. Liz nodded, and the attendant left.

"Liz, why do you drink that stuff? It's not good for you."

Liz growled, "Back off, pussycat." She sipped the gin, swishing it in her mouth, savoring its flavor. "You know, they say gin is suppose to make you horny." She laughed. "As much as I've been drinking this stuff, I should have been laid several dozen times by now." She exploded into uncontrollable laughter at those words.

"Liz!" Toni nudged her.

After sleeping for several hours, they both awakened to the sound of the pilot's voice. "Ladies and gentlemen, if you look to the left of the aircraft, you will see the San Bernardino Mountains."

"I can't see," Toni complained.

"Of course you can't—you're on the right side of the plane, amigo," Liz said grimly.

"Oh, it's good to be back home. I missed the smog, didn't you?" she asked Toni.

Toni didn't respond. She was wondering how she was going to tell everyone the news.

Liz looked at her, "What're you thinking about?"

"Nothing. I'm just glad that we're back."

Downtown L.A. came into view. In a moment they were over Century City.

"Ladies and gentlemen, please remain seated with your seat beats fastened while we make our final descent for landing. This is the captain. We'd like to thank you for flying with us and hope your stay in

Los Angeles will be a pleasant one. The temperature is approximately seventy-five degrees. Once again, thank you for flying American."

The tires screeched, the engines whistled, and the plane began to slow. Liz peeked out the window. "Wow! Look at that smog."

chapter thirty-two

Going Home to Mom & Dad

LIZ AND TONI ENTERED THE terminal and followed everyone to the baggage claim area for their luggage. "You want me to ride home with you?" Liz asked.

"No, I'll be fine. You go ahead. You have to go all the way to Newport Beach. For me, Ladera Heights is only fifteen minutes or so from here."

"Are you sure?" Liz asked.

"Of course," Toni nodded.

"Oh, there's our baggage," Liz pointed out, then looked at the claim tickets in her hand.

A gentleman who was standing by assisted them in pulling the baggage from the conveyor belt. Liz motioned for a skycap to come over, showed him the claim tickets, and pointed to the bags and suitcases. He packed them on a cart and followed the women outside the terminal. The skycap called a cab for

Toni. The cabbie placed her bags in the trunk and then opened the door for her. She walked over to Liz and kissed her on the cheek.

"I'll call you when I think you've made it in."

Liz hugged her. "I'll be waiting for that call. Tell your mom and dad that I will be up to see them before we leave for Miami. Try to get some rest, sweetheart."

Toni got in the cab and the next moment, the driver pulled away.

☙ ☙ ☙

LESTER AND GINA were so happy to see Toni at the door. They both hugged her. "Let me get your luggage," Lester said smiling. Then they went into the house.

Toni marveled, "Mom, how do you keep this place so clean?"

Gina teased, "You're not here." They both laughed and hugged each other.

Lester pulled Toni towards her bedroom. "Nothing has changed since you've been gone. Just like you left it."

Toni peeked in the room.

"Go on in, it's your room, sweetheart." He smiled.

Toni walked in and the first thing she saw was the old teddy bear her father had bought her when she was six years old. She picked it up and cuddled it, then turned to him. "I remember when you came home with it."

He nodded. "That was a long time ago."

Gina asked, "Honey, are you hungry? What would you like?"

"I'm fine, Mom." She continued looking at things in her room and saw her high school yearbook. Pulling it off the shelf, she opened it and smiled at the faces she remembered. Her smile widened as she saw Norma's picture. She turned to her parents. "Have either of you seen or heard from Norma?" They both shook their heads.

"Honey, why don't you rest? When you get up, I'll have your favorite dish ready for you."

Toni beamed at her mother. "Thanks, Mom."

Lester closed the bedroom door, and Gina went to the kitchen in good spirits, glad that her baby was home. In the living room, Lester sat in his Easy-chair while he fumbled with the remote in an effort to find the channel that the Lakers were on. Toni lay on her back, looking up at the ceiling, thinking, *I can't tell them just yet. It will probably break Mom's heart. Oh, God, please help me.*

She got up and walked into the living room where she saw her dad snoozing. Quietly walking over, she kissed him on the forehead and startled him. "It ain't over till it's over," he said, thinking the game was still on and the Lakers were down by two points. Then he noticed Toni. "Hey, there, kiddie-o, I thought you were napping."

"Jet-lag, Dad. The different time zones can really throw you off. Where's Mom?"

"In the kitchen, I think."

Toni walked to the kitchen to see her mom bending over the oven. *She's so great*, Toni thought. "Mom, can I help you with anything?"

Gina turned around. "Sweetheart, I thought you were sleeping."

"Can't do much of that now. I got to get adjusted to the time change. Whatever you're cooking, it sure smells good."

"Your favorite. Guess what?"

"Oh, Mom, you didn't make a casserole, did you?"

"For my baby—you betcha I did."

Toni hugged her. "You're really the greatest. I'm going to call Liz and see if she made it in. I'll be in the den."

Toni walked into the den, but stopped at the china cabinet first to see the pictures that sat there, staring back at her. She smiled as she noticed the picture of her sitting on a Shetland pony and her dad standing nearby.

Next, she picked up the picture of her mother and father standing together in wedded matrimonial bliss. *They were so young*, she thought. In bold, black-and-white letters at the base of the frame were these inscribed words: "You, me, together, forever—until death do us part."

She smiled at another photo that showed her at age sixteen. Then a picture of her and Norma instantly brought back sweet childhood memories.

chapter thirty-three

Bad News

THE PHONE CONTINUED TO RING at Liz's house. *That's odd,* Toni thought. She hung up the phone and mused for a moment, then dialed again. The phone continued to ring. "Something's not right," Toni whispered. She went back into the kitchen where her mom was making crackling bread. "Mom!"

Gina turned to face her. "Yes, dear?"

"I called Liz's house, but got no answer. I find that quite disturbing. I told her I'd call. She said she'd be waiting for my call. That's not like Liz."

"Oh, honey, I'm sure Liz is OK. Don't worry yourself. Look, dinner will be ready shortly. Why don't you go and entertain your father? I'll be finish here shortly. I'm sure he'd love to hear all about those beautiful girls that have been modeling with you."

Toni sighed worriedly. "OK."

Lester was reading a book as she walked in. "Hey, Dad, what are you reading?"

He held the book up called *Cry for Justice.*

"Is it good?"

"Very interesting, I must say. It opens your mind to a lot of things. I think if people were to read this, they'd have an idea in what direction this country is headed.

"Did you call Liz yet?"

"Yes, but there was no answer."

"Well, you know Liz. No telling what she may be into."

"I'm going to try again in a moment."

Suddenly the phone rang. "I'll get it," Lester said. He answered. "Hello. Yes this is he." Toni stood looking at him. "Are you sure?" he asked the person on the other end. "Is it serious?" Toni's eyes became glued to him. "Okay, thank you for calling." He hung up the receiver gently.

"What is it, Dad?" Toni questioned.

He hesitated. "That was the hospital."

"The *hospital*? Why would they be calling here?"

He walked over and put his arms around Toni. "There's been an accident. Liz is in the hospital."

Toni put her hand to her mouth, fearing that she might scream. Lester hugged her tightly. "It's going to be alright. I promise."

Just then Gina walked into the living room, smiling. "Everybody ready to eat?" Then she noticed the drawn faces of her daughter and husband.

"What's wrong? I didn't cook fast enough?" she said cautiously with humor.

Toni walked over to her and placed her arm around her. Gina looked into Toni's face and saw the tears. "What is it, Toni?" she asked, feeling a knot form in her stomach.

Toni looked back at her father, who just stood with his head hung.

"Mom, Liz has been in a accident."

Gina looked from Toni to Lester. "What kind of accident? Did she fall down some stairs? What she do, bump her head? What kind of accident are you speaking of? Lester, what's going on?"

Lester walked over to her and hugged her. "The cab that Liz took from the airport was broadsided by a fifty-foot tractor trailer. They didn't give all the details, but said it was pretty bad. The driver died."

Gina would have fallen if it had not been for Lester holding her. She looked up into his face. "Oh, Lester, no," she whimpered. Toni was sitting on the sofa crying.

"Look, there isn't much we can do right now. She's in surgery," he said, attempting to be calm and strong for his wife and daughter. "Let's pray that she'll pull through."

Toni went to her room and slammed the door. Gina attempted to go after her, but her husband restrained her. "No, honey, let her be. She needs to be alone right now," he said with a hint of grief. He guided Gina to the sofa, where she sat trembling.

"Lester, what are we going to do? We can't just *sit* here. We must go to her. Please, Lester! We have to do something."

"Right now, there isn't much we can do. After she comes out of surgery, we'll go to the hospital. In the meantime, I'll stay in contact with the hospital. Gina, honey, please don't worry yourself. I can't stand to see you upset. You know your condition."

Stoically, Gina stood up. "Are you ready to eat?"

Lester shook his head. "Not just yet, dear."

Gina looked towards Toni's room. "Lester, this has to be tearing her apart. We really have to be strong for her."

Lester nodded. "I know. But she's going to be fine—she has to. She's got that mixed blood, you know." Then he winked and smiled at his wife.

chapter thirty-four ▬
A Hospital Visit

LESTER, GINA, AND TONI ARRIVED at the hospital that evening. Toni immediately went straight to the admissions desk. "Excuse me," she said, speaking to the admission clerk.

The clerk looked up from her word puzzle booklet. "Yes? Can I help you?"

"We're here to see Liz Bolton. Elizabeth Bolton, that is."

The clerk asked, "Is she a patient here?"

For a moment, Toni found herself wanting to answer in the manner that she knew only Liz would answer. She mumbled to herself, "No, she's not a patient. Just the maintenance supervisor." Instead, Toni answered, "Yes, she is."

The clerk looked at a chart and told Toni to go to the nurses' station down the hallway.

"Thank you," Toni said as she beckoned for her parents to follow her. She felt a little faint. It seemed all hospitals had that distinctive, strong, sanitary smell about them. At the nurses' station, Toni inquired about Liz. A nurse looked at a chart and told Toni to have a seat, and that the doctor would be coming to speak with them shortly. Toni sat nervously. Lester and Gina held hands while sitting in the small waiting area. Toni glanced over to see a magazine that someone had left in a empty chair. She looked closely at the cover. It was her picture, where she was wearing a pricy gown at a recent fashion show. She took the magazine and turned it face down.

A short, heavy-set Hispanic woman who was cleaning nearby smiled at Toni. Toni nodded back with a smile. After that, a middle-aged Indian man wearing a turban and who wore the knee-length, white, traditional physician coat walked over to them, holding a chart. "Excuse me. Are you the Morrisons?" he asked with a slight accent.

Toni stood up. "Yes, we are."

He extended his hand. "I'm Doctor Singh."

Toni pointed to her parents, "This is my mom and dad."

He nodded toward them gracefully, studied Toni for a moment, and thought, *Ah, what a beautiful woman.* He continued to smile. "I guess you're here about the condition of Ms. Bolton."

"Liz," Toni corrected him.

He smiled, "Yes, of course. She's in ICU right now. The surgery went as well as can be expected, so now, we just have to wait—at least until the swelling subsides. Then we'll see how she responds. She experienced heavy trauma. She must be a strong-willed woman. She definitely has some fight in her. I've seen people who were less injured and who just gave up. The trauma that she suffered to the head was extensive. We had to go in and fuse some blood vessels; otherwise, she could have easily hemorrhaged."

"Can we see her?" Toni asked, concern etched in her face.

"She's under heavy sedation and won't recognize anyone at this time. Her progress will be monitored around the clock. If there is improvement—or otherwise—we'll contact you. Of course, you can be reached at the number listed on the chart here, correct?"

"That's correct," Lester confirmed.

The doctor thumbed the chart. "Um, does she have any other family?"

Gina spoke with conviction. "*We* are her family."

The doctor smiled and nodded. "Of course! I was just trying to figure out if she has a blood relative, I mean—"

Toni cut him off. "What you mean is, she's a white woman, and you see a white man and a black woman with a caramel-looking woman talking to you, and you're wondering how this all fits in."

The doctor's eyes widened in disbelief. "I didn't mean that at all. I was purely suggesting that if there was someone who was blood-related and a blood transfusion was needed, we would know who to go to."

Toni had become angry. "You think our blood is tainted or something?"

The doctor stood there looking appalled. "I had no reason to think such a thing. It's totally absurd."

Toni felt embarrassed by the comments she had made. "I'm sorry, Doctor. I was out of line. I had no reason to say that. Forgive me. It's just that we are on pins and needles right now. Please understand."

"Under the current circumstances, I do understand. I can imagine how everyone feels at this point. Look, Ms. Bolton will be receiving the best of care, I promise that much."

Lester stood up and extended his hand to the doctor. "Thank you, Doctor. We know she'll get excellent care." Putting his arm around Gina, he said, "Come on, honey, it's getting late. You need to get some rest." He motioned at Toni. "Come on, sweetheart."

"In a minute, Dad. You and Mom go on to the car. I want to ask the doctor a few questions."

Lester and Gina left.

"Doctor, I'm really sorry for my behavior. Please forgive me. It's just that Liz and I have a special bond."

The doctor walked over and picked up the magazine that was lying on the chair. He looked at the cover, then looked at Toni. "Yep! This is you, isn't it?"

Toni nodded.

"You're as beautiful as your picture. You wanted to ask me something?"

Toni looked him straight in the eye. "Honestly, Doctor, what are her chances?"

"The truth is, I don't know. It really depends on her, how strong her will to live is. If she doesn't start hemorrhaging, her chances are far better than worse. If blood clotting sets in, it could very well be fatal. I just can't give you what I know you want. We'll just have to wait and see. You should go home and get some rest. There's nothing you can do here. Besides, your parents really need you now."

"Thank you, Doctor. You've been very honest. Again, I apologize for my rude behavior."

He smiled, "Apology accepted."

Toni walked down the corridor, unaware of the stares she was getting. Of course, they were all complimentary.

chapter thirty-five

No News

TONI HAD LAY AWAKE MOST of the night after arriving home from the hospital. The morning sun edged through her bedroom drapes. The house was unusually quiet this morning. She wondered if her parents were still in bed. Quietly, she got up and tiptoed to the living room. No one there. She peeked in the kitchen. No one there. She went to the den. No one there. She went to the two guest rooms, knocked, no answer. She went to their bedroom, knocked, no answer. She stood in the hallway. "Mom, Dad, you guys here?" No answer.

After all that, she walked to the front door, opened it, and saw that the Oldsmobile was gone. "Did they go to the hospital to see Liz?" she wondered, stepping out on the porch to get the paper. Mr. Curtiss, the neighbor across the street who was watering his lawn, waved.

"Hi, there, Toni! When you get back in town?"

Toni waved back. "Just the other day."

"Long time no see. Welcome back," he said as he continued watering.

"Thank you," she replied almost in a whisper, knowing he probably wouldn't have heard her anyway. She closed the door and went into the kitchen. Her appetite was becoming strange. She knew why, but dared not speak about it openly, at least for the moment. All she had on her mind now was a banana covered with peanut butter. *What a strange craving,* she thought. At that moment, she saw a posted note on the frig. "Sweetheart, we have gone to church. Be sure to eat something. We'll be back as soon as services are over. Love, Mom and Dad."

Toni took a banana from the fruit bowl, then looked in the cabinet for some peanut butter. She layered the banana with the gooey peanut butter, took a bite, closed her eyes, and savored the peculiar taste. *Very tasty,* she thought.

Next, she went to the phone, dialed the hospital, and waited for a response. After a few seconds, someone answered. "Intensive care unit. How can I help you?"

"This is Toni Morrison. I'm calling to check on the status of a patient, Elizabeth Bolton."

"When was the patient brought in?" the voice inquired.

"Yesterday, sometime in the evening, I believe."

"Just a moment, please," the voice responded.

A few seconds went by, but it seemed an eternity. Toni sighed with impatience. "Ma'am, what was the name of the patient again?"

Toni shook her head in dismay. "Elizabeth Bolton," she replied.

"Please hold," the voice said.

Unbelievable, Toni thought.

"Hello! Ma'am, she's been moved to recovery on the eighth floor."

"Does that mean she's doing better?" Toni asked.

"Ma'am, you would have to talk to someone there in that unit. I couldn't provide that information for you."

Toni asked, "Can you transfer me?"

"Hold one minute, please."

Toni wondered, "How can a system be so complicated? It has to be the people in the system, and *they* think of themselves as professionals."

"Recovery, this is Ellen, how may I help you?"

"My name is Toni Morrison. I'm calling to check on a patient, Elizabeth Bolton."

"What's the patient's name again?"

Toni wanted to scream. "May I speak to your immediate supervisor?"

There was a short pause. "Patient Bolton is in room 841."

"Who is the floor nurse? I need to speak to her," Toni said sharply.

"That would be Nurse Rangel. She stepped out to x-ray. I don't know how long she'll be gone; however, if you'd like to leave your number, I can have her call you back."

"Thank you. I'll just check back later."

Toni hung up the receiver. She really wanted to slam it, but wondered what explanation she would give her parents for doing so if she broke it. She sat for a moment, then got up to go to the bathroom. When she finished, she cuddled on the sofa in the den and browsed through photo albums of herself, dating back to when she won her first beauty pageant. There were about six photo albums filled with pictures of her and other young, aspiring models. Pictures of pageants, modeling sessions, fashion shows flooded her mind instantly. Toni looked at the picture of Paula Capeletti. They competed against each other and were actually rivals for the first few years in the industry. After that, Paula had gone on and become successful in her own right. Last Toni had heard, she was branching off into the film industry. *Good for her*, Toni thought.

chapter thirty-six

Confession Time

Soon, Toni heard the front door open. "Mom, Dad, is that you?"

"You up, kiddie-o?" Lester asked.

Toni walked from the den to greet them. "How was the service?" she asked.

"Fine," Lester said, "except your mom got a little exhausted. You know how she gets when she becomes spiritually emotional."

Toni looked at her mom. She appeared tired and weak. "Mom, let me help you to your room. You need to lie down for a while."

After seeing her mother to her room, Toni came back and sat next to her father. She laid her head against his shoulder. "Dad, how long have you been retired now?" she asked.

"It's been just little over a year. Why do you asked?"

"Do you miss being at work? You know, around the people you've worked with for so long. You're only fifty-seven years old. You're still young. You can start another career. If you found something to do for another twenty years, you would only be seventy-seven."

Lester put his arm around her. "I thought about it several times, but I said after thirty years with the police department, I'd just give this time to your mom."

"I thought for sure Mom would have gone back to work. She only had eighteen years with the state. Why did she leave?"

Lester looked a little troubled. "I asked her to stop working."

"But why, Dad?" Toni pursued.

Lester looked away—far away. "I just wanted her home, sweetcakes; I just wanted her home."

Toni couldn't see the tears in his eyes because he didn't face her.

"You must be hungry. Want me to make you something?" she asked.

"How about a sandwich?" he suggested.

She got up to go to the kitchen when her father asked, "Any news about Liz?"

"I called the hospital. Found out that they moved her to recovery."

"Wow! That's great."

"The nurse that's in charge wasn't there, so I said I would call back later. What do you want on your sandwich?"

"However you make it, that's fine with me, kiddie-o."

After Toni made the sandwich for her dad, she told him that she was going to get in contact with her sponsors to let them know that she wasn't going to finish out the modeling and fashion sessions, at least until Liz got better.

"They won't be upset, will they?" he asked.

"They have other girls that can fill in," Toni answered.

"What about your contract?"

"I have a clause that permits me to cancel all my obligations due to unforeseen circumstances or conditions that are beyond my control until those circumstances change."

"I'm glad you have that. Legally, sometimes those things can get kinda sticky."

Toni sighed, "Dad, I need to talk to you about something."

"Sure, honey. Have a seat and let's have a go at it," he said smiling.

Toni sat across from him. "This is very difficult for me. I'm in such an awkward position. First, I want you to understand, Liz doesn't know anything about this. In fact, you're the first to know. I'm going to really need your advice on this. There are so many things that I'm confused about, but I know there will be decisions that only I can make."

Lester leaned towards her. "Sweetheart, life is full of decisions. We make them all the time. Some better than others. But the beauty of it all is that at least we have a choice. It's important to think things through. Oftentimes when we make a decision about something, we do it on the spur of the moment, or we do it when our emotions are running high, and that's not good."

"Dad I've always known you to be a reasonable person. You're opened-minded and believe for the most part, everything has a purpose. I don't know how this will affect Mom."

chapter thirty-seven

The Cat's out of the Bag

"HOW WILL WHAT AFFECT ME?" Gina asked, standing just out in the hallway. Toni and Lester looked at her.

"Mom, I thought you were sleeping."

"Honey, come and sit down. Toni has something she wants to share with us," Lester said.

Gina went to the sofa and seated herself next to Lester. "What is it, dear?" she asked.

Toni looked from one to the other. She swallowed hard. "Mom, Dad, I'm pregnant." She waited for a response from either of them. They said nothing. Toni asked, "Did you hear what I said?"

Lester scratched his head. Gina bit at her finger-nails. They both looked at each other, then broke into a grin. In unison, they both asked, "We're going to be grandparents?"

They didn't wait for Toni to respond. Lester looked at Gina, "I better start looking for some small Laker jerseys."

Gina said, "Oh no! I've got to get little fashionable dresses for her. You know they have children modeling nowadays. No berets, only ribbons that draw more attention."

Lester pondered, "I think I'll have a basketball unit set up in the backyard."

Toni just sat and watched them. "Dad!"

Lester turned to her, "Yes, sweetcakes?"

"We just talked about decisions."

"Of course, we did. One decision has already been made. We're going to be grandparents. Toni, your mother and I are so happy for you."

Gina eagerly asked, "So, have you set a date for the wedding? When will we meet our new son-in-law-to-be? Where is he from? How long have you two dated? Toni, you never spoke of him before. All this was supposed to be a surprise, right? Wow! We're going to have a granddaughter."

"No, honey, we're going to have a grandson."

Gina pinched Lester. "I bet you it's going to be a girl."

Lester pinched her back. "I bet you it will be a boy."

Gina's eyes widened. "Suppose she has twins. Can you imagine *two* little girls running around the house, pigtails flying everywhere?"

Lester shook his head, "Can you imagine two boys dribbling basketballs all over the backyard court?"

Toni interrupted, "Can you imagine me not having this baby?"

Gina and Lester looked as if someone had just shot them with twenty thousand volts of electricity.

"I may not have this baby," Toni repeated.

Gina looked at Lester as if to say, "What is she talking about?"

Lester ran his fingers through his hair. "You're kidding, right, sweetcakes?"

"Look," Toni said, attempting to find a way to not hurt them, yet wanting them to be a little more reasonable, "I can't have this child. I'm not marrying anyone. There's not going to be a son-in-law. Mom, Dad, this just happened. I'm not in love, nor will I be, with the man I slept with. It was an emotional thing where I just got caught up in the moment. I really don't even know him."

Gina gasped. "You don't know him? How could that be? Honey, you were with him."

"Mom, that's just it. I was with him. We met at the fashion show in New York. I guess he was infatuated with me or something. He convinced me to have a late dinner with him. We chatted. He walked me to my hotel suite. He came by the next night. We drank champagne. One thing led to another. Now it's 'oops.' I didn't know until Liz and I left Hawaii for Australia. I haven't even told Liz. I don't even know how. It just happened!"

Gina smiled, "Well, that's okay, sweetheart. You don't have to marry. In fact, after you have the baby, *we can keep her,*" Gina looked at Lester, "or him, while you continue on with your career. Right, Lester?"

Lester didn't really know what to say. He nodded, "Uh-huh."

"Mom, I'm not ready for a child, at least not now. If this gets out, if the papers, the magazines, or tabloids know, it will destroy me. I would become the laughing stock of the industry. Do you understand what I'm saying?"

Gina looked puzzled. "Honey, I do understand what you're saying, but you mustn't make the baby the scapegoat for what took place between you and this man. Sweetheart, take time off until you have the child. We'll keep the baby. That way, you can continue on with your career. Isn't that the best thing to do?" Gina asked, looking at Lester.

Lester coughed. "I think it's a little premature to start thinking about things that have not quite been subject to thinking them through. What I'm saying is right now, it's important that Toni's health is good. We'll have time to talk about other issues later. After all, we still have to be concerned about Liz. Speaking of which, I think we should go visit her and see how things are coming along."

chapter thirty-eight

Six Weeks after the Accident

Toni arrived at the convalescent hospital greatly anticipating seeing Liz. The doctors had said she was making extraordinary improvements. She was talking, but not quite able to move without the help of attendants. Toni entered Liz's room. She noticed all the flowers and plants in the room that had been brought by well-wishers from the industry and friends alike. She smiled as she observed balloons with smiley faces on them reading "get well soon." She also noticed extremely large cards that melted out, "We miss you and love you." She looked over at Liz, who appeared to be sleeping. Quietly, Toni pulled up a chair alongside the bed so as not to awaken her friend. She decided to read the novel that she had brought with her to pass the time if Liz was asleep. She had just begun to read when

Liz coughed. Toni asked with concern, "Liz, do you want some water?"

Liz opened her eyes. "Water? Hell, no, I need a shot of gin." They both smiled.

"How you feeling, girl?" Toni asked.

Liz rolled her eyes toward the ceiling and sighed. "My butt feels like it's a hundred-pound lead diaper. How've you been doing, angel? I heard you cancelled the rest of your fashion shows until further notice. Why'd you do that? You know you could have gone on and done them by yourself until I got better. Don't stop doing what you got to do on my account."

Toni shook her head. "I just don't know what I'm going to do with you. I see you've had quite a few visitors."

Liz snarled, "Most of them were assholes that I don't even care for."

"Liz, you should be ashamed of yourself. How could you?"

"How could I call them what they really are? These are the same people who tried to ruin your career at one time. The same people that went behind my back and talked about me worse than a dog. Some of the same people who questioned why I had a relationship with you instead of with one of the other girls—who just happened to be white. They can kiss my hundred-pound lead ass. They're phony, pure and simple."

Toni reached over and patted Liz on the arm. "Don't go getting your diapers all ruffled up."

They both smiled. Toni asked, "How much therapy do you get every day?"

Liz pondered the question for a moment. "Oh, about an hour or so."

"Is it helping?"

"They put me in this whirlpool with some kind of muscle traction that pulls on my muscles. For all it's worth, I think it's a waste of time."

"Why would you say that?" Toni looked puzzled.

"Shit! I'm not feeling nothing. Every now and then a tingling will come in my big toe. That's not unusual. I was getting that when I was wearing those tight-ass shoes."

They both laughed. Liz coughed. Toni got up and reached for the water bottle on the stand and positioned the straw to Liz's mouth. "Take a sip."

"Level the bed up in a sitting position. I don't want to choke to death."

Toni positioned the bed where Liz was able to make direct eye contact with her. She sipped on the straw, then closed her mouth as if indicating enough.

"So, how is Mama and Papa Morrison doing?" she asked.

"I guess they're doing alright," Toni mused.

"What you mean you *guess*? You're staying there, aren't you?"

"Yes. But you know how it is."

"No, you tell me, Toni. How is it?"

"Liz, now is not the time to talk about this. It's really not that important. I want you to concentrate on getting better."

"Yeah, right!" Liz said.

"What is that suppose to mean?" Toni asked.

"Toni, face it. I'm not going to get better. At least not to where I'm going to be fully functional."

"Liz, why would you even say something like that? Of course you're going to get better. You've got to. I need you around to keep me on the straight and narrow."

"It didn't help when we were in New York, did it?"

Dumbfounded, Toni looked at her. "I thought that was behind us. So you're still upset about that, after all this time? Liz, it happened; it's over with. It's about now. Not yesterday. Why can't you let it go?"

Liz looked at Toni, her eyes sad and hurt. "I can't let it go 'cause you can't let it go."

Toni smiled. "Of course, I can. In fact, I didn't even give it any thought until you mentioned New York."

"Toni, I'm not the brightest person in the world. I'm not educated with the trappings of a B.A. or

M.B.A. I'm just an ol' German-American gal who knows how to use basic math. Right now, it pretty much all adds up."

"Liz, what are you talking about?"

chapter thirty-nine

Toni Finally Comes Clean

"YEAH, YOU THOUGHT OL' Liz didn't know. I knew. But I wasn't quite sure. I was waiting to see if you would tell me."

Toni's heart began to pound heavily. "You were waiting for me to tell you what?" she asked timidly.

"You had all the symptoms of the beginning stages of pregnancy. Oh, Toni! How could you let that happen?"

Toni lowered her head. She was at a loss for words. She had mixed feelings about a variety of things. Guilt overwhelmed her.

"Look at me," Liz said.

Toni looked up at her, tears streaming down her face. "Liz, I'm sorry. I truly am sorry."

"Do your mom and dad know?" she asked.

Toni nodded. "Yes. In fact, they were very receptive and jubilant—until I told them that I can't have this child."

Liz looked at Toni with a raised brow. "What do you mean you can't have the child? You're not thinking about doing what I hope you won't do? Toni, listen to me. I can understand that you're in a state of shock. Of course, decisions will have to be made, but you want to be rational about those decisions. You must think things through. Don't be overwhelmed by emotions and make a choice that you'll regret.

"I know you're concerned about your career, but that can be put on hold for the moment. I know you're concerned about what the industry might think or even say. The hell with the industry. You got to do the right thing."

"I know. I'm just not sure what the right thing is. Liz, what do you think?"

Liz looked at Toni with sincerity. "Sweetheart, you're going to have to be the one that makes the choice. Ol' Liz can say this or that, and of course, that's how I would feel. But it's not about me. I got enough to worry about right now. I wonder sometimes what would have happened if I had gone in another direction, you know, being married, having kids. I've thought about it a lot. I have no regrets though. I chose the way I intended to go. So, here I am. It would be a wonderful thing for Gina and Lester to have a grandchild they can dote on. Of course, they always will have you, but you're not a child anymore. Ol' Auntie Liz would appreciate having a little one around to help the ol' girl out. Toni, pray about this. Find that inner strength, the fairness of it all. Don't be hard on yourself. Nobody is perfect—God forbid that we were because then we couldn't understand the full meaning of the struggle of life and attempt to correct those areas that need correcting. We wouldn't learn in the process. I believe deep within yourself, you're going to do the right thing."

Just then a nurse came in. "Ms. Bolton, it's time for your medication."

Liz snapped, "Drugs after drugs. I wonder if it's helping or keeping me in my current state."

The nurse looked at Toni. "This is going to make her rest. She may fall asleep."

After the nurse left, Liz motioned Toni with her eyes. "Hey, kiddie-o, the next time you come out, be sure to bring me a shot of gin." Liz smiled as she began to fade into slumber. Toni kissed her on the forehead and left.

chapter forty

The Lure of the Ocean

AFTER HAVING BREAKFAST, TONI DECIDED she would take a drive out to Del Amo Mall. She remembered the many times she and Norma would go window-shopping at various malls over the weekends just to see what new fashions were out. Cerritos Mall, Lakewood Mall, Fox Hills Mall, and other fashion outlets. It was always a fun-filled day for them. People were out shopping in droves; some sat and rested at tables, eating nachos or ice-cream. Young girls laughed and carried on, energized by the stares of young boys. The aroma of fresh-baked pretzels floated in the air.

As she drove down hilly Hawthorne Boulevard, the view of the Pacific made her feel as if she were in an enormously open area speckled with glittering jewels reflecting on the water's surface. The air smelled fresh and salty on the breeze carried in from the ocean. By then, she was only a few miles from Redondo Beach, just west of the mall. She recalled how her parents used to tell her about their walks on the Redondo pier. They would select several lobsters from a tank at a restaurant on the beach and have them cooked while they listened to soft jazz. That was back in the days when the beach had what was known as the "concert by the sea" club. Those were some of the treasured moments that her parents cherished.

Toni passed the mall and headed toward a place that she and Norma would visit during spring break. A moment later, she found herself driving on Pacific Street southbound, heading into the heart of San Pedro. San Pedro had been known for many years as a fisherman's town. It had emerald-green sloping hills leading down to its harbor, the Pacific gateway for many a boat and ship.

Toni noticed the sign up ahead indicating a dangerous curve in the narrow road and an arrow indicating a right turn. As she slowed, she looked to her left to see a sign that read Point Fermin Park. She was surprised to see that several groups of people were there, making it difficult for her to find a parking spot. Everybody seemed to be friendly and enjoying their outing on this fine day.

She got out of the car and strolled lazily toward the chain-linked fence that had a sign forbidding people to go beyond it because of the danger of falling. She had to rise on her tiptoes to peer over to see the cliff dwelling and then several hundred feet below, where jagged rocks and boulders lay. Then her eyes drank in the royal-blue water that reached out forever and ever. Far off, she saw a small boat that appeared to be no more than a speck of paper floating aimlessly on the waves. It looked so peaceful, so serene. It seemed to beckon her to come, promising her peace and tranquility that lay far beyond the horizons of this life. The hypnotic spell was broken by an uneasiness in the pit of her stomach. She wasn't sure if it was because of the pregnancy or her mindset.

"Hello, there!" she heard someone say. She turned to acknowledge a middle-aged black man standing nearby. "The view is so beautiful from here, isn't it?" he asked.

Toni studied him for a moment. He appeared to be relaxed and comfortable. He extended his hand to her. "My name is Thomas Overman."

Toni looked at his hand for several seconds, noticing how smooth his skin appeared and his well manicured nails. She slowly extended her hand. "I'm Toni Morrison."

He smiled, showing evenly spaced white teeth. "Nice to meet you, Ms. Morrison. Do you get up here often?"

Toni looked away for a moment, once again being drawn to the beauty of the ocean. "Not often. In fact, I guess I could really say that I'm just passing through."

He nodded. "You know, as corny as this may sound, being here with this spectacular view of the ocean makes for a pretty picture," he said.

Toni smiled, "The view is incredible."

He nodded again. "It certainly is." Then he looked directly at her. "Are you from around here?"

Toni shook her head, "No, I'm afraid not. Look, it was nice meeting you, but I have to be going." She walked to her car, paused, then turned around to see the man still standing there smiling at her. The next moment found her speeding along the Pacific Coast Highway, going northbound.

chapter forty-one

Robbery in Progress

TONI AND HER PARENTS HAD just left the convalescent hospital after visiting Liz and while en route to the Olive Garden Restaurant, two police squad cars whizzed by with sirens blaring. One police vehicle almost collided with a stalled vehicle in the intersection.

"Wow! That was close," Lester said, almost in a whisper. He looked at Gina, who appeared very disturbed. It was the same look he had seen many times before over the years. Whenever she heard sirens, she would get the jitters. Oftentimes he would find her pacing the house whenever he came home late. She shared the same worries that other police officers' wives had, wondering whether or not if he would return home safely, or would she be informed that her husband was fatally injured in a pursuit or wounded in a shoot-out.

"You okay, honey?" he asked her. She just nodded. He looked in the rearview mirror at Toni. "Sweetcakes, everything OK?"

"I'm fine, Dad" she answered.

They waited only a moment to be ushered to a booth inside the restaurant. A waitress brought them a menu and told them when they were ready to order to let her know. Toni sat just opposite of her parents.

"Mom, Dad, have you ever had the Monsoon Salad before?"

Lester and Gina looked at each other and both started laughing. "What's so funny?" Toni asked.

They both said in unison, "Monsoon!"

Lester scratched his head. "Is that some type of weather salad?"

Toni had to smile herself. After their orders were placed, Lester looked over at Toni. "Sweetcakes, how're you doing? Are you feeling alright?"

Toni smiled, "Why do you ask, Dad?"

"No particular reason. Just want to assure myself that everything is fine."

Gina reached across the table and placed her hand on top of Toni's. "Honey, if you need anything, just let us know. We want you to eat well, get a lot of rest, and don't worry about a thing. Lester, her skin looks so radiant, and her hair looks like it's growing longer."

Toni sighed. "Mom, you make it sound as if I'm six months into the pregnancy."

"Honey, I'm just happy for you. I can't wait till the baby comes."

"Mom, we talked about this already. I haven't decided if I'm going to keep the child. Under these circumstances, I may not consider going full-term."

"Oh, Toni! How could you even consider such a thing? Honey, you've been blessed. We all have."

Just as they settled in for a nice meal, in rushed four men wearing hooded sweatshirts and colored bandanas, waving guns in the air and hollering. All four had a bandana that matched the color of his sweatshirt.

The perp wearing the white sweatshirt yelled, "Don't nobody move! Stay calm and nobody gets hurt. Just follow instructions and when this is over, everybody can continue to enjoy their meals."

The patrons were all in a stupor. Some were looking at each other as if to say, "This can't be for real." Others smiled, believing it was some sort of joke. Of course, there had to be a hidden camera somewhere to record the surprised faces of the people. But one couple looked so frightened, it appeared as if the woman was about to pass out.

One of the hooded men stood by the doorway, another by the employee entrance only sign. He stood brazenly in the entrance yelling, "Don't move. You move—you die."

A different gunman walked in the center of the restaurant and spoke very firmly, but not roughly, "Ladies and gentlemen, this shouldn't take very long. If you cooperate with us, we'll be out of your hair in no time."

He looked around carefully and made it a point to establish eye contact with each patron. Suddenly, a woman at one of the tables began to sob. Another of the gunmen rushed over to the table and yelled at her, "What's wrong with this bitch?"

The man that was sitting with her swallowed hard and said, "She's frightened, that's all. She'll be alright, I promise."

The gunman stared down at the woman. "Be quiet or I'll give you something to cry about!"

The gunman wearing white walked up to his counterpart and said, "If I ever hear you use that word again, I'm gonna bust you right across your chops. There ain't no bitches in here. You understand?"

The other gunman stared at his partner, slightly raised the gun, then dropped it by his side. He stepped back a few feet. His eyes were angry, and his brows rose with resentment. Then the white-hooded gunman yelled out, "Listen up! I'm going to make this short and simple. I advise you to listen very careful. No one has to get hurt. Of course, that's up to you. Don't nobody be a hero."

Gina grasped Lester's hand and looked at him with concerned eyes. Immediately Lester's mind registered back to being a cop. He surveyed the scene. Toni whispered at him, "Dad! You're not a police officer anymore. Please, just take it easy."

Lester continued to ponder the scene as he spoke without referring to anyone in particular. "Once a cop, always a cop."

"Okay, ladies and gents. This is how we're going to play this game," the white-hooded gunman said. "My friend here," nodding at the gunman with whom he had had a slight altercation, "is going to come to each table with a bag. What you're going to do is simple. Take your wallets, purses, rings, watches, earrings, and put them in his bag. Very simple. No fuss. No deliberating."

The gunman in the red-hooded sweatshirt walked to each table with the bag open, waiting for each patron to drop in the items that had been requested of them. The gunman who wore a blue-hooded sweatshirt yelled to no one in particular, "Hurry, man! We got to get out of here."

A woman sitting at a rear table struggled to get her ring off her finger. She pulled and prodded, but the ring wouldn't bulge. The gunman stared at her.

"You want me to cut off that damn finger of yours?" he snarled.

The woman looked at him with pleading eyes. "I'm trying; it just won't come off."

The gunman looked at her with disdain. "That's what happens when your fat ass eats too much. By the time I get to the other tables and get back here, you better have that damn ring off, or I'm going to take your whole arm."

The woman worked furiously in an attempt to get the ring off. The gunman arrived at Toni's and her parents' table. His eyes fell directly on Toni. "Wow! You're a beautiful lady. I think I'll let you keep whatever you have."

He reached towards Toni to stroke her face. Lester leaned forward. "You touch her, and I'll break your face."

The gunman turned to Lester. He stared at him for a long moment. "Oh, we got us a hero. Look, pops, take a deep breath, relax, and live."

Lester looked at the gunman with such a menacing look that it made Gina shiver. Lester and the gunman continued to stare each other down.

Finally the white-hooded gunman yelled, "Move it, man. We got to go."

The gunman looked at the ring on Gina's finger. "Oh, that's nice. Let's put it in the goodie bag."

Gina started to pull at the ring on her finger when Lester said, "Keep it on, honey."

The gunman looked at Lester in disbelief. "Are you stupid or what? I want that damn ring, and I want it *now*."

Lester immediately stood up. "You want it? You got to go through me."

The gunman looked almost surprised. He raised his gun with the one hand and pointed it at Lester's head. "You want to dance with me, big man? Can you do the boogie? How about a waltz? Yeah! That's it. Let's waltz, you and me. Let's make some music."

"Stop it, please!" Gina almost cried out. "Lester, honey, please, it's not worth it."

Lester's jaws tightened. "It's worth it to me. No ring, Elmer Fudd. Do what you gotta do."

The gunman shook his head. "You're one crazy sonavabitch. All just for a ring."

The white-hooded gunman yelled, "We're out of here. Move it!"

The gunman at the Morrison's table paused, looked at Toni, winked, and said, "I hope we meet again—of course, under different circumstances."

The gunmen fled the establishment, with the last one stopping to take a bow towards everyone.

chapter forty-two

Turmoil Builds

SEVERAL DAYS HAD PASSED SINCE THE incident at the Olive Garden. One of the suspects had been picked up on another robbery attempt. Lester was still fuming, wishing he had done more. Gina stood behind him as he sat in his Easy-chair, massaging his shoulders. "Honey, you did what you could under the circumstances. They had guns. I'm grateful that no one got hurt. Thank God they didn't know you were a retired police officer."

"Gina, I think I recognized one of them. The one that was at our table. His eyes. I saw those eyes before, Gina."

Gina stopped with the massaging. "Where, Lester? When?"

"I think it was someone I arrested a couple of years back. You know I always had this thing about a person's eyes. The eyes tell you a lot. The eyes let you see into the soul, Gina. Good or bad, the eyes are revealing. After the police arrived, I told one of the fellows that possibly this guy may be one of the culprits. They're going to check it out. By the way, where is Toni? Haven't seen her all day."

"She found out where Norma is staying and went to visit her."

Gina sat next to Lester. "Honey, I'm worried. Toni has been acting rather strange lately. She seems so distant at times. I'm really worried about her, Lester."

Lester took Gina's hands and placed them in his own. "Honey, she's probably experiencing a lot right now. The pregnancy, her career, Liz's condition, and God knows what else. She knows we'll be there for her if she needs us. She probably just needs some space, time to think things through. You know she can be tough as nails when she has to. Let's just give her the room that she needs."

"Lester, you don't think she'll do anything rash do you?"

"Rash? In what way, hon?"

Gina shrugged, "I'm thinking about the baby. What's going to happen? She seems set on not having the child as part of her life. Oh, Lester, I want that baby to be a part of our lives. It would be our first grandchild. Isn't there something we can do to assure her that it's the right thing to do?"

"Gina, we have to let her make her own decisions. I'm sure she'll come around. If we press her, she may distance herself further from us. Let's just try to be supportive of her. Sounds like she just pulled in the driveway. Come on, honey, look pleasant. We don't want her to think that something's wrong. Why don't you go and prepare something to eat."

Toni entered the house. "Hi, Dad."

Lester smiled. "Hey, sweetcakes. How're you doing? Heard you went to see Norma. How's she and her family?"

"Oh, Dad, I had such a great time. Norma hasn't changed a bit. She works as an executive assistant for a law firm in Century City. We went out to have a bite to eat and talked about old times. It was a blast."

"Did you tell her the good news?" Lester asked.

Toni looked surprised. "What news?"

"About you, sweetheart—the baby."

Toni looked away from him. "No, I didn't. I hoped I didn't even look revealing. Dad, I can't tell her just yet. I don't feel comfortable about it. Why is everyone making such an issue of the situation? It's no big deal. Exactly what's going on here? I feel like there's a conspiracy going on to make me decide to do what others want me to do."

Lester rose from his chair. "Of course not, honey. Why would you think such a thing?"

Toni walked away, went to her room, and closed the door.

Lester followed her and knocked on her door. "Toni, sweetheart, I didn't mean anything about that. Please come out and let's talk. Honey, you know I would never say or do anything to hurt you. Please, baby. I apologize if I spoke out of line."

Toni just lay across her bed, tears flowing down her cheeks. At that moment, she felt totally alone. There was nothing or anyone that could possibly make her feel that tomorrow would bring sunshine.

Gina stood in the kitchen doorway. "Lester, what is it? What happened? What's wrong with Toni?"

Lester stood silent for a moment. "She needs space, Gina; she needs space."

Gina felt weak in the knees. She steadied herself by leaning against the wall. Lester walked over to her and put his arms around her waist. He helped her to the sofa. "Honey, are you alright?" he asked worried.

Gina didn't answer. She looked pale.

"Gina, what is it?" he asked.

"I just need to rest," she said in a whisper.

Lester looked concerned. "Maybe I need to take you to the doctor."

She managed to shake her head. "No, just let me rest for a moment."

Lester took one of the sofa pillows and propped her head up. He rubbed her hands gently, looking at her affectionately. "Baby, is there anything you want me to do?"

She never answered. In a matter of seconds, Gina had closed her eyes and fallen asleep. Lester stared at her. His eyes moistened. "God, please, give her more time with me. I can't go on without her." The tears came freely down his face. He, too, felt alone at that moment.

chapter forty-three

Toni Hooks up with Norma

THE PHONE RANG. TONI SAID, "I got it. I'm expecting a call from Norma. Hello?"

"Toni, it's me, Norma. What's up, girlfriend? Are you busy?"

"No, actually, I was just sitting here reading. What's up?"

"I thought maybe you would like to go and see a movie. I hear that movie *And the Rain Came* is suppose to be pretty good."

"What time did you have in mind?" Toni asked.

"There's a showing at 8:15. The movie is about two hours and twenty-five minutes long."

"That's fine, Norma. You want me to pick you up?"

"No, I'll come by your way. We can go to the Century Plaza Theatre. I should be at your place about 7:30."

"Sounds like a plan. I'll see you then, girlfriend. Bye."

Toni went to her room to change into a pair of baggy pants and an oversized sweatshirt. Then she went into the kitchen and scooped a spoonful of peanut butter. "Um," she said, as the flavor of the peanut butter smeared all over her tongue. She looked in the pots that sat on top of the stove burners. Her mother had cooked some vegetables, rice, and baked some chicken in smothered mushroom sauce. Toni frowned—not that the food was unappealing. It was her taste buds that were whacky. Pickles, peanut butter, cherries with cream cheese were her delicacies of choice these days.

She walked out to the backyard to see her mom pruning flowers and pulling up weeds. "Hi, Mom. I see you're doing a little gardening. The roses look beautiful."

Gina smiled as she continued pulling up the weeds. "These weeds try to choke off everything. You really got to get to them before they become too strong. How're you feeling? You eat something?"

Toni studied the sky. "I'm OK. Is it suppose to rain? It looks cloudy."

Gina paused for a moment and looked up at the sky. "It does appear overcast. I hadn't really noticed until you mentioned it. You going somewhere this evening?"

"Norma and I are going to the movies. Have some girl-bonding. Hey! Would you like to come with us? It will probably do you some good to get out and enjoy some evening air."

Gina pricked her finger on a thorn from one of the rosebushes. "Ouch!"

"You alright, Mom?" Toni asked.

"You got to be real careful with these roses. As pretty as they are, they will make you believe that beauty is in the eye of the beholder, not the hand," she smiled. "Where's your father?"

"I think he went to the auto-parts store for something. He should be back shortly."

Gina stood up and sighed, "I never knew how much work it took to keep flowers groomed. I feel like I've been on my knees for hours. I think that's enough for now. I may finish up tomorrow."

She laid the garden spade on a small table, took off her gardening gloves and laid them aside. "I guess I'll go make your father something to eat."

"Mom, you already cooked. Did you forget?"

"I sure did, didn't I? My! What am I thinking?"

Toni looked at her very curiously.

"What time is Norma suppose to be here?"

"She said about 7:30."

"Where are you girls going?"

"To the movies, Mom. Didn't you hear me tell you that just a moment ago?"

"I know, but what movie theater?"

"We're going to the Century Plaza Theater."

"You're going way over to Century City? Isn't that a little out of the way? Magic Johnson Theater is just across town."

"Mom, we chose Century Plaza. We may also want to browse around at the stores."

"Well, you both just be careful."

Gina entered the house going directly to the kitchen, where she washed her hands, took the water pitcher from the frig, and poured herself some in a glass. Then she drank the water quickly.

"Mom! Slow down. You're drinking that so fast someone would think that you just completed a twenty-mile marathon."

Just then the door opened. Lester came in holding several bags. "Been shopping, I see," Gina said smiling, knowing he would always do what was needed to be done to keep that old Oldsmobile running.

"Had to get a few items for the Olds. If I keep it serviced and maintained, that old girl will run forever. Who knows? She might outlast me."

He looked at Toni, "Going somewhere, sweet-cakes?"

"Norma and I are going to the movies."

Lester nodded. "Good for you girls. You haven't spent that much time together since you've been back home. Enjoy!" he said, as he left, going out the back door to the garage.

Gina followed him asking, "Lester, are you ready to eat?"

"I'm fine," he called back. "I'll be in the garage for a few minutes. Go rest yourself, sweetheart."

Gina stood with her arms folded, staring at the garage. Toni stood watching her mom. She could see the love she had for such a husband. Toni knew that they were no good without each other. The years had bonded them well. She walked to her mother and kissed her on the cheek and squeezed her. Just then a car horn blew. Toni walked over to the window and peeked out. It was Norma.

"Mom, I got to go. You and Dad be sure to get to bed. I don't know exactly what time I may be in, so don't bother waiting up for me." Toni grabbed her waist-length jacket and put it on. Gina walked to the door and stood there as Toni exited.

Norma waved, "Hi, Mother Morrison. How you doing? Tell Dad I said hello. I love you both. See you in a little bit."

Gina waved at her. "You girls be careful. Make sure your doors are locked. Don't drive too fast and be sure to buckle up."

Toni and Norma looked at each other and giggled. "It's almost like old times when we were back in high school," Norma said, backing out of the driveway.

She paused for a moment, searching in the console for a CD. "Ah, I found it," she said.

Toni looked at the CD. "I didn't know you like Alicia Keys."

Norma smiled, "I like the Dixie Chicks too."

chapter forty-four

Second Thoughts

It was 10:30 p.m. when Norma dropped off Toni at her parents' house. "Hey, girlfriend, I had a nice time," Norma said.

"I did to," Toni replied as she got out of the car. "Call me when you get the chance. Maybe we can go and have brunch somewhere when you're free."

"You got it, girl," Norma said. "Anywhere will be find—except the Olive Garden," she laughed.

Toni pointed her finger at her, smiling. "No stopping at strange places on the way home."

"Girlfriend, the only place I want to stop that is no stranger to me is my bed. I'll call you. Take care. Bye."

The house was dark when Toni entered, with the exception of a dim light coming from the den. She tiptoed into the kitchen, opened the cabinet, and pulled out the peanut butter jar. Using a spoon, she dipped it in the jar and pulled out a hefty amount of the gooey spread and stuffed it in her mouth. Then leaving the jar on the counter, she walked into the den, turned on the TV, channel surfed, and found a station that was showing late-night movies. Licking the peanut butter spoon, she debated with herself about going back to the kitchen to retrieve the jar. "Naw," she said and within twenty minutes, Toni had dozed off. Images began to appear in her head. In her sleep she asked, "What do you want from me?"

A voice replied, "I just want to love you."

"You don't even know me," Toni said.

"I know you. You carry me within you," the voice responded.

Toni awakened to find herself perspiring. She went to her room, undressed, and looked at her stomach to see the little bulge. Running her hand over her stomach, she spoke, "Little one, oh, little one. What am I to do? You're a part of me; yet strangely, I don't think I'll ever come to know you. We both will have a long journey ahead of us."

Unbeknown to Toni, Gina was listening to what Toni was saying just outside her bedroom door. She had heard Toni talking to herself when she was about to go to the bathroom. At the time, she wasn't sure if someone else was in the room or not. She was trembled hearing Toni say, "I don't think I'll ever come to know you." Those words sent a cold chill down Gina's spine. After using the bathroom, she quietly slipped back to her bedroom.

She stood over Lester, gazing at him while he snored in blissful slumber. Troubled, she went to the living room and sat on the sofa in the dark as she clasped her hands together, looked at the ceiling, and began to speak. "God, You brought this wonderful man into my life. You blessed us with a beautiful daughter. You have given me the best years of my life. I'm thankful for all the wonderful things I've had. Only by Your will I've been able to come as far as I have. I know if You want me to beat this breast cancer, then Your will be done. I ask, though, please, let Toni make the right decision about this baby. Let her know that this is a gift, in spite of the circumstances that caused the child to come into being. Forgive her for her shortcomings, but guide her to do the right thing. God, thank you, again and again." Gina wiped the tears from her eyes as she went back to bed.

chapter forty-five ▬

The Accident

LESTER HAD JUST PULLED INTO the intersection when a car ran through the red light and broadsided him. The impact pushed him nearly onto the sidewalk near a flower shop. He sat there, dazed for a moment in an attempt to clear the cobwebs from his head. People were running over to the scene of the accident. The car door was jammed. Finally it gave way when he heaved forcefully. As he exited the car, someone said, "Are you alright, mister? Do you need help?" Lester looked to see a heavy-set Hispanic lady staring at him with wide-opened, shocked eyes. Her Spanish accent was heavy, yet her English was good enough for him to understand when she said, "Mr.! Me call 911 for you, sí?"

"I'm fine," Lester said. "But thank you very much."

He looked around and saw the other car, but no driver. To no one in particular he asked, "Is the other driver alright?"

The Hispanic lady who was still nearby said, "Him get out of car and run away."

The other car was pretty much disabled. The grill was hanging loose, and it appeared the radiator was punctured. Steam hissed beneath the hood as water leaked out. Lester looked inside the vehicle and saw an open bottle of whiskey on the seat. The smell of alcohol permeated the air. By then, Lester heard police sirens in the distance. He walked back to his car and retrieved his registration.

The little, heavy-set Hispanic woman again asked, "Mr., you OK? Me see blood on your head." She pointed to her own brow to indicate there was a cut or abrasion on Lester's head.

He dabbed at it with his forefinger and saw that there was a little trickle of blood. Paramedics had arrived on the scene followed by a police vehicle. Once the scene was surveyed and there appeared to be no life-and-death situation, the paramedics looked at Lester's cut and covered it with a bandage. "You won't need any stitches. Just the first layer of skin's broken. Are you hurting anywhere else? Back? Neck? Shoulders?" the paramedic asked.

"I'm fine," Lester remarked. "Just a little shaken, but I'll be OK."

The paramedic nodded. "If I were you, I'd go to the hospital to get some x-rays. You know, to be on the safe side."

"Thanks, but I'm sure I'll be just fine."

The police officer came over and asked Lester what had happened. After explaining and the officer wrote down the information, he asked Lester for his phone number in case he needed to be contacted further. "If you lose the number, just ask any of the guys at Metro if they know Lester Morrison."

"Why would I do that?" the officer asked.

"I worked Metro and Newton for quite a few years," Lester replied, revealing his retirement badge.

"Oh, really? Ex-cop, huh? I'll tell the fellows I bumped into you—excuse the pun. Can you give me any information about the driver of the other car?"

Lester shook his head. "Nothing other than it appeared to be a hit and run. He fled the scene. Probably would have driven off in his vehicle had it not been disabled. Did you notice the alcohol bottle inside it?"

"Yeah. I got a tow to hitch it up and take it to impound. You need tow assistance?"

"Naw," Lester said while looking at the Olds. "That ol' girl can take a licking and keep right on trucking."

The police officer shook Lester's hand, then Lester climbed into his car. It cranked up immediately. He knew when he arrived home Gina was going to question him about everything so he pulled the bandage from his brow. She would panic if she saw it. He put the car in gear. It jerked for a moment, then drove off as if it had just stopped to get a breath of air.

chapter forty-six

It's All in the Head, Liz

Liz screamed, "Will *somebody* get in here?" She struggled to move but was unable to.

A moment later, a certified nurse's assistant arrived. "What's the problem, Ms. Bolton?" she asked.

Liz rolled her eyes. "The problem is, I just *shit* on myself."

The nurse smiled. "You did a boo-boo, huh? Well, we'll just have to get you cleaned up. We can't have you laying around, stinking up the place now, can we?" The nurse was being sarcastic. Liz mumbled under her breath, "Bitch! If I could move, I'd kick your ass from here to eternity."

Liz had pretty much given the staff a difficult time since her arrival at the convalescent hospital. "I'll be right back," the nurse assured her. "I have to go and get something to clean you up. You wait right here. Don't you go nowhere." The aide left, smiling.

Liz gritted her teeth. After she was cleaned up, she strained to look out the window, then heard voices and wondered who it was. She asked herself, "Why me? What have I done to deserve *this*?"

Her thoughts were interrupted by Dr. Mason. "How're we doing today, Ms. Bolton? You look lovely as ever."

Liz stared at him. "Bullshit!"

The doctor smiled, "That's what I heard. You had an accident a moment ago, didn't you?"

"Why don't you cut the crap, Doc? Just lay it on me straight. Am I *ever* going to walk out of this place?"

Doctor Mason fumbled with Liz's chart. "That all depends on you, Liz."

"If it depended on me, I'd have been long gone. Hell, I can't even move. What's up with that?"

Doctor Mason smiled. "Liz, you can't move 'cause you're not ready to move. It's in your head, Liz—your head. The muscles can't do anything until you activate them by way of using your mind."

Liz laughed. "You got to be kidding. You think I've been lying here all this time 'cause I like being bedridden? Doc, there's a lot of things I'd rather be doing, believe me."

Doctor Mason walked to the bedside and lifted Liz's hand. He massaged it tenderly. "Do you feel any sensation?"

"No, but if you were to massage somewhere else, I bet I would," she laughed.

Doctor Mason continued massaging her hand. "When you recover, you might want to become a comic. I think you're a natural."

Liz looked down at her hand. "Am I suppose to feel something? 'Cause if so, guess what? I wouldn't even know that you were holding my hand if I didn't look to see."

"Concentrate, Liz. Get out of your head that this was suppose to happen. You have to free yourself from the force of complacency and guilt."

"Guilt? Me? What did I do? I wasn't driving that big rig. I was a passenger in a taxi. Why should I feel guilty about anything?"

"I don't know, Liz. Only you can answer that question," Doctor Mason replied. "Search, look deep into your mind. There's something that's not letting you go forward."

Liz smirked. "I thought you were a medical doctor, not a psychologist?"

"Sometimes you have to be a little of both, especially when you're trying to get people back into life's stream."

Liz sighed deeply. "Maybe some people don't *want* to get back in life's stream." Sometimes the pain, the sorrow, the anguish, the deferred hope become too much to bear. Maybe the wound is too deep to heal. Too much out-patient service, not enough of intensive care—you know what I mean? Too many Band-aids, not enough stitching. Do you understand what I'm saying, Doc?"

"You're absolutely right, Liz, however, healing won't begin until the patient recognizes his need of *wanting* to be healed, to continue in life's stream."

"Look, Doc, whatever I have to do to get out of this damn bed, I'm willing. Money sure didn't help. I must have spent a small fortune by now."

"You're going to have therapy in an hour or so. Think about what I said. It's in the head, Liz—all in the head. I'll be around to see you this evening. By the way, can you take it easy on the staff a little?" He smiled and left.

Liz mumbled, "The staff needs to take it easy on *me*. Damn! I wish I could have a drink of gin."

chapter forty-seven━
Toni Moves Out

LESTER AND GINA WERE UPSET when Toni told them that she was going to Hawaii, at least until she had the baby. By this time, she was seven and a half months into the pregnancy.

"Lester, what did we do? Did I say something to offend her? Why would she just get up and go like that? Lester, I'm afraid. Oh, God, please don't let anything happen to her or the baby. Maybe we should go to make sure she's alright. She might need something."

Lester looked into Gina's worried face. "Honey, calm yourself. You're getting all worked up. It's OK. She's going to be fine, I promise. She had to do what she had to do. We could not have stopped her if we wanted to. That's the decision she made."

"It just doesn't make sense. Something's not right," Gina said, pacing the floor.

"Gina, please. You're putting me on nerve's end," Lester complained.

"I won't rest until I find out, Lester. What's going on? I sense something. It's just not normal."

"Gina, listen to me," Lester insisted. "Toni has to go her own way. Whatever she does, it's her decision and she has to live with it."

Gina looked at Lester sternly. "What about *me*? What about *you*? Don't you think *we* deserve to have some say in all this?"

"No!" Lester said sharply. "We need to stay out of it. She'll bring us in when she wants."

Gina pointed her finger at Lester, something she had never done before. "You don't *want* a grandchild. You were just trying to appease Toni. Of all the nerve! Maybe it's time for me to do some rethinking. Maybe I've been blind all along, all of these years. Maybe I'm seeing you now for who you *really* are."

"Gina, you're talking very foolishly. You're not being rational at all. Why don't you sit down and relax. You're getting yourself all worked up over nothing. Don't make yourself sick, please!"

"I wouldn't be surprised if you went behind my back and persuaded Toni to do this. How could you do this to me, Lester?"

Lester went to her in an attempt to calm her, but she pushed him away. "Don't touch me. Don't ever touch me. You've used me. You've destroyed me." Gina went to their bedroom and slammed the door.

Lester was at a loss for words. His head was spinning, going round and round. "This is not real," he was trying to convince himself. He knew it wasn't a dream because he wasn't sleeping. He walked to the bedroom door where he heard Gina crying. He wanted to go in, but felt it was best to just wait. His palms were sweaty as he rubbed them together. He needed to do something, but he didn't know what, so he paced back and forth. He stopped near the phone and thought of calling Toni, but realized it would only make things worse. Toni would be upset because Gina was upset. Gina would become even more upset, fearing that if Toni became upset, it would cause the baby to be upset. Then everybody would be upset.

Lester hadn't taken a drink in ten years, especially after becoming a full-pledged member at his church. He sure thought about having one now, though. Serious thought. Instead, he grabbed the keys to the SUV. "I'll go for a drive," he said to himself.

"Naw, if I'm gone and Gina doesn't know where, she'll become even more upset."

So he went out to the garage and just sat. For the first time in his life, he felt vulnerable, exposed, and bare. "This can't be happening," he mumbled.

He thought how he and Gina had first met. He was only twenty-three years old, just out of the police academy. A still-wet-behind-the-ears rookie cop. Gina had driven through a stop sign. He was with his field-training officer when they pulled her over. The training officer told him to handle the situation while he observed. After issuing her a citation, he had apologized to her.

"For what?" she asked in surprise. Her smile had dazzled him. He had never seen such a beautiful black woman before, except maybe in the movies. She, too, saw something in his eyes that she had never seen before. She felt awkward about the situation. *He's white,* she thought.

His thoughts were interrupted with, "Lester, Lester, are you there?" He recognized Gina's voice.

In an effort to go to her, he scraped his hand on the saw blade that was lying on the workbench. "I'm here, Gina," he said as he made his way to the back door.

He saw her standing there with tears streaming down her face. "Oh, Lester, I'm so sorry. Please forgive me."

He embraced her tightly. "I love you, Gina. I've always loved you. I never will stop loving you." He lifted her head and kissed her on the lips, then whispered, "Forever, forever, and forever."

chapter forty-eight

The Hideaway

Toni had found a nice little rental near the beach. It was almost secluded. She liked it very much, offering her the privacy that she needed for the time. The baby moved. "You like it too, huh?" she asked while rubbing her hand across her stomach. Leaning against the wall, she looked out the window to the deserted beach just beyond. The cool, tropical breeze gently blew through the door she had left open. She fought back tears that threatened to spill because of the guilt that she felt. She knew her parents were heartbroken. Her mom almost went into cardiac arrest when she found out that Toni was leaving. Toni didn't like doing this, but felt it was necessary. She didn't want the chance of being outright exposed. She knew how the media would react to her pregnancy. If they were to find out that she gave birth, it would be a free-for-all, no-hands-barred, major media frenzy. She wasn't ready for all the drama that came along with the privilege of being a celebrity model. She whispered to herself, "I'm sorry, Mom. I had to do what I had to do."

She thought about calling her parents, just to be sure that they were alright, but decided otherwise, believing time would work out everything for the best. One of the island regulars who helped Toni move in stood at her open door, knocking.

"Renee, I'm going to the market. Would you like me to pick up anything for you?" he asked.

"No, I'm fine. Thank you, Fu-Fu," Toni replied. It seemed so strange that she was called by her middle name. Under the circumstances, though, she felt it would lessen the notoriety associated with her celebrity status by just being plain ol' Renee, the island girl. Of course, whenever she went out, she would always disguise herself, often wearing wigs and dark shades. "It's only for a little while," she told herself. She remembered telling her dad what she intended to do, but didn't dare tell her mom, knowing she would be in total disagreement. *Dad understands. At least, he pretended to anyway.* She knew that if he disagreed with her mother, there just might be hell to pay. Toni loved her mom dearly, but felt there were times that she could be so unreasonable. Next, her thoughts flew to Liz. "I guess I could have called her," she reasoned. But Liz had enough problems already. There was no need to weigh her down with someone else's.

As the sun began to set, it gave off a beautiful fiery-orange reflection on the water. At that very moment, Toni did feel like she was in paradise. Everything seemed so serene and peaceful. She decided to give herself a pedicure, so she went to the bathroom to retrieve the foot tub. She was looking forward to soaking her feet in warm water.

Seating herself on the sofa with her feet planted in the crystal-filled water, she turned on the TV. The local news station was airing a breaking-news event that had just taken place off the coast of Spain. A plane had crashed carrying a hundred and ninety people. Images from the crash showed debris and smoke billowing from a portion of the plane's right wing. Another image showed emergency personnel looking for survivors. The news anchor said, "An update on this tragic event will be forthcoming."

Toni turned to another news station, only to hear that two Americans that had been passengers on the plane were affiliated with the fashion industry. Toni's heart began to pound. *Oh my God!* she thought. She waited to see if the names of the victims were given, but they had not, pending notification of kin. She turned the TV off and immediately stood up, forgetting that she had her feet in the water. She almost stumbled forward, but was able to grab the arm of the sofa to steady herself. She stepped out of the foot tub, not bothering to dry her feet. Then she walked to the phone, but paused and just stared at it, trying to decide who she should call. Then conflicting thoughts came. *I don't want anyone to know I'm here other than my parents.*

She went back and stood in front of the TV, wanting to turn it on, yet afraid of what she might possibly learn. She wasn't ready for anything that would disturb her bliss, as this news already had.

chapter forty-nine

Working Things Out

THE PAINS WERE SHARP AND at times intense. *It's way too early,* Toni thought to herself. *I'm just in my eighth month.* She attempted to reason with herself that she could have possibly miscalculated, or the baby was merely hinting of an early exit, saying, "I'm ready to make my grand entrance." Toni swallowed hard and breathed deeply. The pain subsided, but she felt a push on her uterus. She swallowed again. *This is strange,* she thought. No sooner had that thought crossed her mind, the pain came again. This time it moved in her back like a flaming arrow. This was followed by another pain in her side, a sharp and jagged one. She managed to climb out of her bed and walk over to the dresser to get her cell phone. Scrolling down, she searched for Fu-Fu's number. He had told her if she needed him for anything to be sure and call him. He was only minutes away, spending most of his time at his "Welcome to Ha-waii/Tourist Guide Attractions" office.

Fu-Fu had been living on the island for more than ten years. He knew everything there was to know about anything when it came to the islands. Though he was of Samoan ethnicity, he felt all islanders were the same. After being discharged from the military, he came and set up shop here, making a living by being a tourist guide and a handyman. He could fix just about anything, and he was always pleasant. He offered to help anyone in distress. He had helped Toni find her rental cottage and moved her in. She smiled as she thought about how he came up with his nickname, Fu-Fu. He said when he was a small child and was hungry, he would go to his mom and wrap himself around her leg and say, "Me want fu-fu," meaning he wanted food. Toni imagined how cute that must have been. Finally, she noticed that the pain had subsided except for a mild tingling in her side.

She turned to the mirror and examined herself. *I haven't really picked up the weight that I thought I would. My face is a little fuller and my dimples a little deeper, that's all,* she thought.

Three and a half weeks had gone by since she had arrived at the island. Her thoughts went back to Liz's condition. She wanted to call her, but dared not. She was sure that by now, her parents had told

Liz what she had done. Toni needed time to work out what she wanted to do after having the baby. She needed to be as secretive as possible. She definitely didn't want the media and the industry personnel to get ahold of this.

She had already contacted and spoken with a representative from an adoption agency. A young couple had been put on a waiting list to receive an infant female child. The woman was unable to have children. She and her husband had been waiting for close to two years since they had initiated the process of adoption. There were so many hoops to jump through, so much red tape involved. This couple had responded with interest after being told by the agency that a young single woman who was career-oriented was considering giving her baby up for adoption. Little information was given to the couple about Toni, leaving her celebrity status and full name out of the conversation. However, the couple was told that the child would be coming from a fine heritage. They didn't mind that the child was biracial, as long as she was a healthy baby.

Toni felt all the pressure of decision making. She knew what she wanted to do, but was confused in what direction she should go. The thought of her parents learning that she had given up their grand-child was almost unbearable. She knew it would affect her mom physically. Her dad would conceal the hurt. He would only say, "It's your decision, and you're the one to have to live with it." Liz probably would tell her, "You're such a jerk, short of being an asshole." *What would Norma say? Why did Norma have to know?*

If the industry did find out, how would they re-act? All these thoughts swirled around Toni's head. Her head began to throb from all the tension. She wanted someone to talk to. But who? There was no one at the moment that could console her. She thought of calling Fu-Fu. "No!" she said aloud. She only would call him if she really needed him. She felt a walk along the beach would ease the tension, so she placed a shawl around her shoulders and exited the cottage. She was about fifty yards from her place when the phone rang. However, she was so immersed in her thoughts, she didn't even hear it.

chapter fifty-
Bad News

AFTER RETURNING FROM HER STROLL along the beach, Toni settled in for a peanut butter sandwich and a glass of milk. She put on a CD and listened to the romantic sound of Alicia Keys. As the music filled the room, her mind drifted. For a brief moment, she wondered about Jean Plushette. More than likely, he was somewhere attempting to hit on some young girl with his charm and bedroom-seducing eyes. *So strange, she thought. A one-night affair, a moment of lust, brought me to this point in my life.* Her physical and emotional needs had been out of control. She pondered the questions: Is my career over? Can I ever again regain my place in the modeling and fashion world? Is there any hope, or am I just fooling myself? Only time would tell.

The phone rang. Toni hesitated to pick it up. "Who could possibly be calling?" she asked herself. "Who knows that I'm here other than Mom and Dad?" the phone was relentless. Finally, she reached for it and said, "Hello?"

"Toni, it's Dad. I'm sorry, honey, I know it's not probably a good time, but I had to call."

"Dad! I'm so glad you called. I was really beginning to feel desperate."

"Are you OK, sweetcakes?" Lester asked.

"I'm physically OK; I'm not sure about my mental state, though."

"What's the problem?"

"I just got a lot of things on my mind. I hadn't realized all the difficulty that this was going to cause. I know you told me that I would have to make decisions; that's why I decided to leave, for the most part. I figured if I isolated myself, it would be easier to come to terms about things. I can imagine how Mom must feel. I'm so sorry. But Dad, I know you can make her understand. You've always had that way of making her see things plainly. By the way, how's she doing?"

"Sweetcakes, I want you to sit down, if you're not already sitting. I called to let you know that your mother is in the hospital."

There was a long pause.

"Toni? Toni? Baby, are you alright?" Lester asked with concern in his voice.

Finally he heard Toni's voice, which seemed like light years away. "I knew it. I just knew it. It's all my fault. I shouldn't have been so selfish. What have I done?"

"No, no, baby, it's not you. I had promised your mother a long while back that I would never tell you. She made me promise. I tried to tell her that you should know, but she said she didn't want anything to interfere with your career."

"What is it, Dad? What didn't Mom want me to know?" Toni asked impatiently.

"Toni, your mom has breast cancer."

The phone dropped from Toni's hand. Lester yelled into the receiver, "Toni? Toni, baby, speak to me!"

There was a sharp pain. The baby kicked hard.

part ii

I Won't Cry If Tomorrow Comes

THE EXCITING CONCLUSION TO THIS stirring novel is forthcoming. A sneak preview reveals the following:

Toni spent countless hours investigating, searching, seeking to find where the adoption agency had placed her child. She was bent as hell in turning over every stone, every pebble, to find the gift that she had given away. Her time was running out. She was beginning to panic. She didn't even know her own child's name.

Toni went back to Dr. Richards, her physician, for a status update on her blood disorder. She feared the worse, but was relieved when Dr. Richards told her after having additional tests done, he found that her white blood cells were multiplying.

"What does that mean?" she asked.

He smiled. "What it means, Ms. Morrison, is that you're going to live. You don't need a donor. The medication you've been taking has halted the disease. There is marked improvement. You can start celebrating."

Tears formed in the corners of Toni's eyes.

"My dear, that's something worthwhile to cry about," Dr. Richards stated.

But Toni's tears weren't tears of joy. The real pain was just beginning to set in, as she thought, *Oh my God! My baby!*